Elizabeth leaned over to her desk and easily located the paper she wanted. She scooted her mug to one side and placed the list on the TV tray. "Can you see all right, or do you need more light?"

"I'm afraid I can't see as well as I used to." William scooted his chair closer to hers. "But I'm fine if I get close enough to what I'm trying to read."

"Let me show you some of the things I've found."

As they leaned together over the list, William's handsome left side was all she could see. Suddenly she shivered. She was being drawn to him like a magnet to steel, just the way she'd been when they had first met, and now, just like then, she couldn't stop herself. He was so refined and fascinating . . . so polite and . . . and . . . appealing. He was everything Tom wasn't. Smooth, wealthy, brilliant . . . and he smelled so inviting.

William leaned closer. Elizabeth closed her eyes and enjoyed the sensation of William's warm breath tickling against her cheek . . . her neck. She was like a cold, shivering creature being invited into a soft, warm cocoon. His hand accidentally brushed hers, and her heart fluttered nervously.

"Elizabeth," he whispered, leaning even closer.

Moistening her lips, she waited expectantly for his kiss.

Bantam Books in the Sweet Valley University series.
Ask your bookseller for the books you have missed.

And don't miss these Sweet Valley
University Thriller Editions:

Visit the Official Sweet Valley Web Site on the Internet at:

http://www.sweetvalley.com

SWEET VALLEY UNIVERSITY®

THRILLER EDITION

Deadly Terror:

The Return of William White, Part II

Written by
Laurie John

Created by
FRANCINE PASCAL

BANTAM BOOKS
NEW YORK · TORONTO · LONDON · SYDNEY · AUCKLAND

RL 8, age 14 and up

DEADLY TERROR: THE RETURN OF WILLIAM WHITE, PART II

A Bantam Book / February 1999

Sweet Valley High® *and Sweet Valley University*®
are registered trademarks of Francine Pascal.
Conceived by Francine Pascal.

Produced by 17th Street Productions,
a division of Daniel Weiss Associates, Inc.
33 West 17th Street
New York, NY 10011.

ISBN: 0-553-49262-4

Published simultaneously in the United States and Canada

Bantam Books are published by Bantam Books, a division of Random House, Inc. Its trademark, consisting of the words "Bantam Books" and the portrayal of a rooster, is Registered in U.S. Patent and Trademark Office and in other countries. Marca Registrada. Bantam Books, 1540 Broadway, New York, New York 10036.

PRINTED IN THE UNITED STATES OF AMERICA

OPM   0 9 8 7 6 5 4 3 2 1

To Diana McNelis

Chapter One

Elizabeth Wakefield gazed into the shadows at the edge of the Sweet Valley University quad as a form slowly materialized. Male . . . tall . . . well built . . . It was hard to make out much since he was dressed all in black.

She shivered. Only one person she'd ever known dressed that way, but it couldn't be him. He was dead.

A breeze rippled the branches overhead, allowing a ray of sunshine to penetrate the shadows for a moment. In the sunlight the figure's white blond hair and pale complexion practically glowed.

Elizabeth's breath caught in her throat as his profile flashed into view. It couldn't be . . . but it was! Her worst nightmare, back from the dead . . . William White.

No. This was just a nightmare. Wasn't it?

She reached up to her face, expecting to feel

1

virtual-reality headgear, but it was gone. Moments ago she'd been stuck with William in a twisted fantasy, an all too lifelike cybernightmare. But even then the dream had ended with William White falling over a cliff. He should have been just as dead in her fantasy as he was in real life.

But all week William White had seemed far from dead. Visions of him had haunted her. He'd chased her through three traumatic virtual-reality fantasies, and she'd even begun seeing him around campus. Of course it was never really him. The person would always be some innocent bystander who just happened to have blond hair and an aristocratic attitude. One time it had been her boyfriend, Tom Watts, who had accidentally frightened her.

She rubbed her eyes. Maybe she was suffering from some sort of aftereffect of that last awful CyberDream session. Yes, that had to be the answer. The William standing before her was simply a figment of her imagination.

She sighed tiredly. Was virtual reality like some hallucinogenic drug that would give her frightening flashbacks for the rest of her life?

For days she and her friends had been in the clutches of Jonah Falk, a bizarre cross between a carnival pitchman and a dark genius. He'd brought the CyberDreams Virtual Reality Fair to campus, promising experiences that would reflect the cyberdreamer's innermost dreams and fantasies. True, he had warned everyone not to take it too far. But had he known all along that the CyberDreams would become more and more addictive until they crossed over into real life?

Elizabeth glanced over her shoulder. The quad was deserted and quiet. The gigantic Cyber-Dreams tent and its accompanying gray-purple clouds were gone, as if they had vanished into thin air. She and her friends should be safe. But apparently not. How long were these awful effects going to linger? How long before she would quit having these nightmares? Would her life ever get back to normal?

She frowned back at the image of William and willed it to disappear. It only stood there in the shadows, staring back.

She placed her hands over her eyes. If only she'd never seen that awful white rose on the CyberDream sign, thoughts of William would never have occurred to her. White roses had been William's calling card. Thanks to him, the very sight of a white rose would give her goose bumps for the rest of her life.

She opened her eyes again and faced the dreadful hallucination. She willed it to vanish, to disappear. But instead of disappearing, William stepped closer. If anything, he seemed to become more concrete, more real. And he was holding a long-stemmed, white rose.

Elizabeth raised one hand to her mouth in horror.

She held the other out in front of her, as if to ward off evil.

Without a word, William shoved the flower into her outstretched hand. Elizabeth's fingers closed instinctively around the stem.

She cried aloud as a thorn stabbed her finger. She stared at the offending flower in disbelief. A dream wasn't supposed to hurt.

Nearly in shock, she watched numbly as her own blood formed a scarlet bead. Warm. Wet. Sticky. It dripped down onto the grass at her feet. Real blood.

She shuddered. Surely this was a dream. Surely she was going to wake up . . . now.

Elizabeth blinked and shook her head. She felt bleary, tired, and short of breath, as if she had just woken up from a nightmare. Yes, that *must* have been what happened. When she looked up from the ground, she would see no William White. Nothing but trees and shrubs and grass and blue sky.

She was wrong.

William White still stood there before her, silent. He kept his head turned to one side. His lashes, so long that they practically rested against his cheek, were just as she remembered them. The sun caused the diamond earring in his left earlobe to sparkle. His chest rose and fell with his audible sigh.

Elizabeth gasped. She stumbled backward a couple of steps.

"Don't be afraid," he urged quietly. "I'm not here to hurt you."

"But—but you're dead!" she gasped.

He held his arms out to his sides and posed dramatically. "As you can see, I'm not."

"But I saw you die! We had a wreck and you hit—"

"Elizabeth, I regret what I did to you so much that sometimes I wish I *was* dead."

Elizabeth's heart pounded. She wished he was too—more than anything.

He held out one pale hand toward her.

She wanted to scream, but her throat felt as if it were stuffed with cotton. She wanted to run, but her legs felt mired in mud. She could only stare . . . and wait.

He stepped closer. "I'm so very sorry for everything. Can you ever forgive me?"

"Forgive you?" she cried, reclaiming her voice. "You—you say that like you forgot to send me a birthday card or you bailed on a date or something."

William shook his head. "I won't trivialize your pain. I know how horrible I was, and I've come to apologize for . . ." He moistened his lips with his tongue. "For everything."

Elizabeth swallowed the lump in her throat and stared at his calmly handsome profile. Once they'd dated. But after she'd exposed him as the head of a racist secret society on campus, he had stalked her mercilessly. He'd terrorized her, leaving threatening notes and mutilated dolls in her Jeep and in her room. But that had been only the tip of the iceberg. How dare he minimize his evil deeds!

"You did more than stalk me, William. And you know it." Elizabeth practically spit her words in his face. "You tried to kill me. You were locked up for it, and before I had time to relax, you escaped and . . . and you set up my ex-boyfriend, Todd, for car theft and murder. You tried to kill my best friends! You . . . you tried to kill me— *again!* You're in—"

Elizabeth clamped her teeth over her bottom lip. She suddenly remembered what had happened the last time she'd called William White insane. It had nearly cost her her life.

Quickly she met his gaze. Had he caught her slip of the tongue?

William eased out of the shadows.

"Don't take another step," Elizabeth warned. "If you come any closer, I'll scream!"

He stopped and wiggled his fingers, palm up, beckoning. "Don't be afraid of me, Elizabeth. I'm not the same William who I once was. I'm fully aware of all the pain I've caused you, but I have done penance for each and every evil deed, believe me."

Elizabeth's mind whirled. Penance? He *was* crazy! "What kind of penance does one do for attempted *murder*, William?"

6

Without comment, William eased still closer.

Run! her brain screamed, but her body wouldn't obey. Standing under his icy blue gaze, she felt as helpless as a vampire's victim, hypnotized before the final bite.

"My penance is written all over my face," he said. Slowly he stepped into full sunlight and turned his whole body toward her until his entire face was visible.

Elizabeth gasped. The whole right half of William's face was a shapeless bulge covered with the shiny, fiery red scar tissue of a burn victim. His right eye, hardly more than a slit between the swollen folds of flesh, was gray and rheumy.

It was disconcerting to see both sides of his face at the same time. The perfect symmetry of his left side seemed almost mocked by his right. When she first met William White, she'd thought he was the most beautiful man she'd ever seen. And from the left side he still gave that illusion. From the right he was a monster.

"Pretty awful, isn't it?" he asked casually.

"What hap—" Again Elizabeth clamped her mouth shut. She didn't have to ask what had happened. She knew very well. Sometimes she still had nightmares about William's silver Kharmann Ghia flying over a cliff with her in it. It was a miracle that it hadn't. That had been precisely William's plan, until she'd grabbed the wheel and run them off the road and into a tree. She'd

7

escaped virtually unharmed—physically anyway. William hadn't been so lucky. She could still remember the deathly crunching sound of his body slamming against the windshield during the wreck—the wreck she'd caused.

She glared. He deserved exactly what he got! Why shouldn't he look like a monster? He *was* one. But as she continued to stare at his ruined face, her softer side came to the front. Tears of pity filled her eyes. Elizabeth couldn't bear to think that she'd caused such ruin to any living creature. *I did that,* she thought. *I've ruined William's beautiful face.*

Her pity ebbed, replaced once again by fear. For ruining his face, he hated her more than ever. A cold chill of realization skittered up her spine. He had come back to kill her—to make her pay for doing this to him!

Without taking her eyes from his, she began to back away.

"I know what you're thinking," he said.

"Y-You do?" she stammered, freezing in place.

"You're thinking that with all my money, I could have had plastic surgery. That there's no excuse for my going through life looking like a freak. But you're wrong."

"I—I am?" Her knees weakened with relief that he hadn't actually guessed what she had been thinking.

"I'll admit, I had the very same attitude at first.

8

You know how vain I always was. But after two surgeries, this is as good as it got." He laid his palm on his scarred cheek. "It took me a while, but finally I came to the realization that this hideous mask was a just punishment. My constant reminder of the evil monster I'd become." He dropped his gaze to the ground. "It's what I deserve. I'll wear it to the grave."

Elizabeth looked down at her feet. William was being too reasonable, too calm. He was up to something.

"Look at me, Elizabeth. It's because of this"— he pointed to his deformed face—"that I've changed. I'm a totally new man. Believe me."

"Why should I believe you?" Elizabeth's voice came out in a frightened croak. "Give me one reason why I shouldn't go to the police right this minute and have you locked back up in jail— where you belong."

William seemed to shrink back as if stung by her words, but he recovered so quickly, she thought she might have imagined it. He resumed a more arrogant stance. "You will *never* turn me in!"

Elizabeth gasped.

"Sorry, I didn't mean to shout." William lowered his voice. "I'm not afraid that you'll turn me in, Elizabeth . . . because you're too softhearted. You can't help it. It's just the way you are. I know you. You believe that all people are basically good inside. Even me."

She shook her head.

"Is it so impossible to believe that I've retrieved that goodness I was born with?"

"I—I don't believe you. You're trying to trick me."

"Elizabeth, you loved me once. Surely there must have been something worthwhile in me for someone as honest and good as you to see it."

Elizabeth chewed on her bottom lip. She hadn't loved him, had she? She'd been having that argument with herself all week. She hated to think that she'd been such a poor judge of character. But it was true—she *had* been terribly attracted to him when she'd first come to SVU. She'd thought that he was the most handsome, smart, sophisticated, perfect man she'd ever met. But that was before she got to know him.

"I didn't love you," she insisted. "I could never love you!"

"Please, Elizabeth. It kills me that you could look at me with such horror in your eyes. I thought if anyone would understand and give me a second chance, it would be you."

Elizabeth wanted to look away, but she forced herself to stare right at the injured side of William's face. His scar tissue was as unyielding as a mask. No signs of emotion of any kind. As she watched, William's lashless, half-opened right eye filled suddenly with moisture. A tear slid slowly down the scarred flesh of what had once been a masculine but rosy, soft cheek.

10

Overwhelmed, Elizabeth turned away. She waited a moment to catch her breath and get control of her emotions, but when she looked back up, William had vanished.

She blinked furiously and swallowed back a scream. Where had he gone? She looked left and right. Not far away she saw students crossing the quad as if it were any ordinary day. A butterfly flitted past, and she could smell newly mown grass. What was happening to her? Had she been dreaming? Hallucinating? Or was William a part of her new, horrible reality?

No choice was a good one.

She looked down at the delicate rosebud, which she still clutched in her hand. Her own blood stained its creamy white petals.

She dropped the flower and fled for her dorm.

Tom Watts opened his eyes to a blur of bright green and blue. He squinted his eyes shut, then tried again. Slowly a canopy of green leaves swirled into focus. He closed his stiff fingers together and felt soft, damp . . . grass? Weird. He was lying flat on his back on a smooth lawn. Had he fallen asleep while studying on the quad?

He blinked a few times. Overhead, through the leafy branches of an oak tree, he could see patches of a perfectly blue sky. The purplish gray storm clouds that had hovered above the campus for days had disappeared. He felt like Rip Van Winkle waking up in a new world. A painful new world, he realized, as feelings slowly returned to his numbed body. He felt stiff, sore . . . and his head ached.

"W-What happened?" he muttered. The sound of his own voice clanged in his ears and sent a sharp pain from his eyes to the back of his head. He gingerly touched his forehead. What was he doing here? He tried to concentrate. He hadn't been studying. He could remember that much. He'd been running . . . running toward his girlfriend, Elizabeth, when suddenly everything had gone black.

"Elizabeth!" he called out, struggling to raise himself on one elbow. Just the small movement of lifting his head from the ground caused it to throb with pain.

He strained to remember. Elizabeth had been running from the CyberDreams tent as if a demon were after her. He needed to rescue her—his damsel in distress . . . no. That was his virtual-reality dream . . . or was it?

The CyberDream had left him completely confused and disoriented. He couldn't tell what was real and what was a dream anymore. Was that why he'd passed out?

Tom pushed himself off the ground with his arms, waited for a wave of dizziness to pass, and then sat up. Cradling his aching head in his hands, he tried again to sort out what had happened.

His CyberDream had been set in medieval

times. He'd been a knight, slaying dragons and witches—always in the pursuit of rescuing a lovely blond princess. In his first two visions he'd assumed the princess was Elizabeth. But in his third dream the blonde who had finally turned to reward him had no face.

Tom shuddered now at the very memory, but at the time he'd nearly freaked. Especially after that creep Jonah Falk fed him some line, claiming that the virtual-reality dreams were merely generic, prerecorded minimovies. One was chosen for each participant, and the dreams were only personalized when the viewer's imagination filled in the faces. Falk had tried to convince him that the faceless princess was Tom's own problem. It meant he didn't know who he really loved. Ridiculous! Tom knew exactly who he loved. He loved Elizabeth Wakefield—the Elizabeth he'd seen running from the tent in fear—

And if she was running in fear, then she must have been in some sort of trouble. He had to get to her . . . help her . . . even if he couldn't quite remember why.

Keeping one hand firmly against the tree trunk, Tom pulled himself to his feet and came face-to-face with a low-hanging branch. Evidently in his mad dash across the quad he'd run headlong into a tree limb and knocked himself out. He winced as the blood pounded against his skull. *What a klutz,* he thought.

He glanced around the quad to see if anyone had witnessed his clumsiness, but the whole place was deserted. Even the CyberDreams Virtual Reality Fair tent had been removed. *How long have I been unconscious?* he wondered with amazement.

Dark spots began to dance before his eyes, and he grabbed the branch for support. Was it the blow or the aftereffects of that stupid virtual-reality episode? That Falk character had warned him not to visit the tent more than twice, but he'd been suckered back—hooked by the idea of being a hero. The call of the fantasy world had been too strong to resist.

Three times he'd visited Falk's ridiculous mind-manipulating machine—each time getting more involved in his fantasy and more removed from his reality. And to what end? It'd left him with a brain full of cobwebs. Had it affected Elizabeth the same way? Was that why she'd been running away in terror? If he could only get to her, he could find out. They could comfort each other, work past this grisly episode, and get back to normal.

He took two wobbly steps before a white light exploded in his brain. Raising his hands to his ears, he held on until the wave of nausea passed. Again the lump on his head throbbed with a stabbing pain. Tom reached up and touched it.

That's weird, he thought, staring at the crusty, brownish blood that came away on his fingers. If he had run headlong into a tree branch, then why did he have an egg-size lump on the *back* of his head?

William White took another deep, cleansing breath and relaxed against the soft cushions of the couch. They had become so familiar to him that their very feel and smell made him feel safe. He'd spent a lot of time on this couch over the past few weeks, and he had the routine down pat. At least this time the therapy was helping. It was nothing like his experiences with psychotherapy in the past. In fact, as much as he hated to admit it even to himself, it had become his salvation. His frequent talks with Dr. Denby were the very thing that was bringing him back to reality.

From his reclined position he stared at the dim light overhead for a moment and then closed his eyes.

"Shall I turn out the light, William?" The calming voice of his psychiatrist, Dr. Orrin Denby, floated over him, soothing him.

"No. It's OK. It's not too bright after being outside."

Dr. Denby was the best psychiatrist William had ever had. And for William, that was saying a lot. In his lifetime he'd seen more psychiatrists than most people see movies. But no matter how rich, famous, or recommended they had been, none of his other doctors had ever understood William the way Dr. Denby did.

Take the matter of the light, for instance. Dr. Denby knew that William preferred to hold these therapy sessions in semidarkness. Not only was it easier to talk in the dark and deal with his mangled face, but bright lights hurt his bad eye. No one else seemed to care about his feelings, but Dr. Denby always had.

"Did you see Elizabeth as you'd planned?"

"Yes. Yes, I saw her." William squirmed, suddenly bursting with the need to talk. "She is still so beautiful, Dr. Denby. Like an angel . . . even more heavenly than I remembered."

"But I sense you're unhappy," Dr. Denby observed.

"Miserably." William ran a hand through his hair. "She's an angel, but there is no forgiveness for me in those aqua eyes. I'm afraid it's hopeless. I've done too much damage to her soul."

"You mustn't give up. Don't you want release from your inner pain?"

William sighed. "Of course I do, but it's no use. She will never forgive me. I was a fool to have ever believed that she would. Even the CyberDreams didn't convince her that I've changed. That whole gambit—it was all just a waste of time and money. Almost the last of my money. If anything, I believe she's more frightened of me than before."

"But in time she'll forget—"

William jumped up. "No. No, she'll never forget what I've done!"

Dr. Denby gave William a stern look of warning.

William lowered himself back to the couch, but he sat on the edge of the seat, his spine stiff. He didn't like interrupting Dr. Denby. The doctor was an extremely smart man, usually full of insights and advice, but he wasn't getting the full picture in this case. He hadn't been out on the quad. He hadn't seen the horror in Elizabeth's eyes. When William had revealed his deformed face to her, she'd been so appalled that tears had come to her eyes. Every tear she'd shed felt like a razor blade slicing into his heart.

"William," Dr. Denby began. "You're getting worked up. Take a deep breath and relax. Feel the peace. You're safe here with me."

William did as instructed and felt the muscles in his back unclenching. "I'm sorry," he said after a couple more deep breaths. "I'm just so disappointed. I thought I'd waited long enough, but she is still scared of me."

"Why do you suppose she's afraid?"

"I don't know." William stared at the overflowing bookshelf. He couldn't meet Dr. Denby's knowing stare.

"William, you're in denial. You must face the reality of what you've done before you can understand Elizabeth's fears. And you have to understand Elizabeth's fears completely if you hope to move beyond them."

William didn't want to rehash the past. He'd

been through it all so many times, but he knew Dr. Denby wouldn't let him rest until he cooperated. He took another deep breath and held up his index finger. "First of all, she still thinks of me as the plotting, scheming person who led that neofascist secret society on campus."

"Go on."

William held up another finger. "Second, she sees me as the person who stalked her."

"Simplified, perhaps, but OK. What else?"

"I—I tried to kill her friends." William dropped his hand to his side, no longer wanting to keep track of his crimes. "I couldn't help it, Dr. Denby. I had nothing against those people, but they were stealing her from me. I couldn't stand the thought of sharing Elizabeth with anyone. I wanted them out of her life once and for all." William sank back onto the couch. "But that was then. I'm a new person now."

"You aren't finished with your list."

"Yes, I am," William insisted. He waited. When Dr. Denby said nothing more, William raised his head and looked at the doctor's face. It was closed off, totally uncommunicative. Dr. Denby wasn't going to allow William to proceed until he admitted his worst sin.

"All right . . . I'll admit it," William confessed. "I tried to kill Elizabeth once."

Dr. Denby remained quiet.

"OK, twice. I tried to kill her *twice*. But that

was the old William, who was crazy with desire and obsession. I said I hated her, but I really did it out of love—misguided as it was. I was driven to it by the fear of losing her and the pain of her rejection." Unable to go on, William threw his arm over his eyes.

"William, you're doing very well. Don't sink back into despair. Don't undo the progress we've made."

William opened his eyes, raised himself up on one elbow, and faced the psychiatrist. "I'm sorry, Dr. Denby. I'm still weak. I'm afraid there's no hope for me. Without Elizabeth's forgiveness, I don't want to go on." William dropped back against the sofa.

"I truly believe she *will* forgive you, William," Dr. Denby said. "From everything you've told me about her, I feel I know and understand your young lady very well. Though she may not forgive easily, she's the type that forgives completely. You mustn't give up hope. If she is as strong a person as you say she is, then her forgiveness could very well be the key to your recovery."

"Oh, she is."

"You will simply have to convince her that you've changed."

William buried the right side of his face in the pillow. "Oh, she's seen how I've changed!" he wailed.

"That you've changed *inside*, William. Don't fixate on your disfigurement."

"I try not to, but sometimes I can't help but think about it. I know I look like a monster. No one could ever love me."

"Of course someone will. There are people in this world who don't judge people by their outer appearances."

William disagreed, "Only a saint could love someone as deformed and ugly as I am now."

"Or an angel," Dr. Denby reminded him.

William felt his hope returning. "Yes, an angel. A beautiful, brilliant, blond angel."

"Your Elizabeth is a rare find. You know very well that looks aren't important to her."

"Yes," William agreed. "She's one of the few people in the world who sees beyond the surface to the person beneath."

"Then don't be afraid to let her see you. The real you. The inner you. Do you think you're ready?"

William cracked his knuckles and stared at his fingers.

"William? Have I ever given you bad advice?"

"No. Never."

"Then tell me how it'll be."

William leaned forward and met Dr. Denby's gaze. "Once Elizabeth sees how I've changed, then she'll forgive me."

"And once she forgives you?" Dr. Denby prompted.

"Once she forgives me, then I can move on to the ultimate level."

"Which is what?" Dr. Denby asked.

"You know. . . ." William fidgeted and began plucking threads from the frayed edge of a cushion.

"I agree that Elizabeth's forgiveness is essential to your recovery since she was the focus of your, uh . . . obsession."

William leaned back and threw his arm over his face again, shutting out the light and muffling the sound of Dr. Denby's voice. He *hated* that word! It reminded him of the time he had been called insane. . . .

"William, are you listening to me? I think I should know what you're planning."

William shook his head like a stubborn child.

"Come on, William. Tell me what's on your mind. We should talk about this."

William burrowed deeper in the cushions. Even though Dr. Denby had been his closest confidant for months—in fact, his *only* confidant—William wasn't so sure he was ready to let Dr. Denby in on his biggest secret. His fingers closed around the cushion, and he squeezed it tightly. "I think we're about finished for today, Dr. Denby. Aren't we?"

Chapter Two

Jessica Wakefield groaned and stuck her fingers in her ears. "I'm not at home," she shouted at the jangling phone.

When the racket finally stopped, she rolled over on her stomach and angrily flicked through the pages of a fashion magazine. The blasted phone had been ringing off the hook all morning, but she was way too angry and embarrassed to speak to anyone. She was still fuming over that CyberDreams rip-off.

Last week, bored and temporarily between boyfriends, Jessica had hoped she might get something going with that cyberhunk Jonah Falk—until she found out what a creep he was. He'd smiled and flirted like crazy, leading her on. But the whole time he'd been playing her against her sorority sister and very worst enemy in the whole world, Alison Quinn. It'd all been a humongous waste of time.

The phone started ringing again. Jessica tossed down her magazine, crossed over to the phone on her sister's desk, and angrily switched on the answering machine. "There!" she snarled. "Talk to someone who cares!"

She'd hardly had time to stretch back out on her bed when an alluring "hello" sent shivers up her spine. The sexy male voice sounded familiar, but she couldn't quite place it.

"I'm trying to locate the Jessica Wakefield who used to go to Sweet Valley High," the voice continued. "If I've reached the right number, Jess, would you please return my call? This is Charles Sampson, and for the next three hours I can be reached at two-one-three . . ."

"Charles!" Jessica squealed in disbelief. Charles Sampson was an impossibly gorgeous film director she'd met years ago—back when she was still a junior in high school. He'd stopped her one day when she was biking near Sweet Valley Beach and asked if she'd ever considered being in the movies. She'd thought it was a come-on at first until he'd explained that he'd seen her guest appearance on the soap opera *The Young and the Beautiful*. He was convinced that she'd be perfect for the part of Blythe in his movie *Checkered Houses*.

Even though she'd had to eventually turn down Charles's movie offer in order to salvage her relationship with her high-school boyfriend Sam Woodruff, she'd gone out with Charles several times. They'd become friends, and she'd secretly helped him raise financing for his movie. Charles had been so grateful, he'd even dedicated his movie to her.

Hurrying to get to the phone, Jessica got tangled in her balled-up comforter and then tripped over a pile of books on the floor. By the time she snatched up the receiver, all she heard was a dial tone. Never easily deterred when she was on the trail of a gorgeous man, she replayed the message, scribbled Charles's number on one of Elizabeth's notebooks, and dialed it immediately.

Charles Sampson! She hadn't thought of him in ages, but now that she'd been reminded, she could hardly wait to talk to him again.

"Hello, Charles?" she blurted the moment she heard the line open. "This is Jessica—"

"One moment, please," a well-modulated female voice interrupted. "I'll put you through."

Jessica smacked her hand against her forehead. Of *course* Charles would be important enough to have a secretary now. He was famous. *Checkered Houses* had been the surprise hit of the season, and Charles's picture had monopolized the covers of movie magazines for months. In fact, now that she thought about it, he'd been on the cover of the new *Hollywood Buzzz* she'd bought last week. Where had she put it? She began rummaging through a pile of papers on her desk as she waited for Charles to answer.

"Jessica?" came his voice at last. "Is it really you?"

Jessica took a deep breath and tried to sound calm and sophisticated. "Charles, dear. I was just coming in the door from uh . . . a luncheon date at the country club . . . when I heard your message on my machine."

"How great to hear your voice. I was afraid you wouldn't remember me."

"Oh, I remember *you*, all right!" How could she forget? She had practically fallen head over heels for him. If she hadn't been so terribly in love with Sam at the time, who knew where she and Charles might have ended up. "I never forget the men I spend the night with," she added jokingly.

"If I remember correctly, you weren't very happy about that night."

When Charles's beautifully restored, vintage Mustang had broken down on their way home from a secret trip to film mogul Martin Pederson's home in Santa Barbara, she and Charles had been stranded on a lonely road. They'd been forced to spend the night in the car, waiting for a passerby to rescue them. And even though Charles had been a perfect gentleman, it had still almost cost Jessica a boyfriend!

"I hope you're not still going to hold that against me," Charles joked. "I got rid of that car as soon as we made it back to civilization, by the way."

"I can't say I'm too disappointed." But actually she was. The very thought of being stranded with Charles on a romantic back road made her pulse flutter with excitement. And why shouldn't it? She was totally unattached these days and a lot more mature.

"I guess you've heard about how well *Checkered Houses* has been doing?" he asked.

"Heard about it? I've seen it *ten* times!"

"As long as it took to shoot and edit, I was beginning to think I'd never get it released. It's been what, two years?"

"Well, I'd say it was worth the wait. I loved how you put that dedication to me at the end of the credits."

"It was the least I could do. I'd never have gotten Martin Pederson to back me if he hadn't been so impressed with you."

"Oh, I don't know about that," Jessica said, trying to sound modest.

"It's the truth, and you know it. You are the one who saved my pet project—even if you did refuse to be my star. Ginger wasn't half the Blythe you would have been."

"Oh, right. Only every critic in the country raved about your sister's performance."

Charles laughed. "Well, you already know what I've been doing the past two years, so how about you? Been doing any acting lately?"

Jessica giggled. "Not unless you count acting

innocent when my sister catches me coming in late."

"Sounds like not much has changed."

Actually a million things had changed since high school, but she was sure a rich Hollywood director wasn't going to be interested in college life. The important thing was, Charles hadn't seemed to change. He still sounded as friendly and open and charming as he had two years ago. And since she was presently between boyfriends, Charles's timing had definitely improved.

"So why have you never called me?" she asked in her flirtiest tone.

"You mean, aside from the fact that you told me never to call you again?"

"Oh yeah. I forgot. But surely you have a better reason than that."

"Actually, I figured you were probably married with a couple of towheaded kids running around underfoot by now," he joked.

"Well, if that's the case, then what suddenly changed your mind?"

"The funniest thing, Jess." His voice dropped the kidding tone, and he suddenly sounded more serious. "I was in Disc-Oh! Music this morning and I picked up this calendar of sorority women on the beach. Saw this girl on the cover—looked just like you, but I couldn't be sure. So there I was, nonchalantly flipping through it, admiring the babes, and then I got to Miss December. I nearly popped a contact. There you were, real as life, in that fire-engine-red bikini with the Santa hat—more gorgeous than ever, I might add."

Jessica glanced at herself in the nearest mirror and smiled. She was proud that a professional like Charles recognized her modeling talents. "It was a charity gig. All the sororities on campus were clawing to get a spot. I was just lucky to be chosen." Actually Jessica had used all her feminine wiles to get a spot in the prestigious calendar, but she was still trying to maintain a hint of modesty. "So, are you calling to get me to autograph my calendar picture?" she asked with a laugh.

"The real reason I called, Jess, was because I need a favor."

Jessica dropped into Elizabeth's desk chair as her soaring hopes suddenly descended like a lead balloon. "What favor?" she asked suspiciously.

"Come on, Jessica. For old times' sake."

She sighed loudly enough to let him know she wasn't pleased. "OK," she said. "I'll help if I can. What do you have in mind?"

"Have you ever heard of the IM Awards?"

"The Independent Movie Awards? Sure. Who hasn't? I still keep up with the industry, although I'm *totally* committed to my education right now. But I guess once the acting bug gets in your blood, you can't shake showbiz."

"I know what you mean. There are a couple of

things I've never been able to get out of my system either."

"Movies and . . . ?"

"Your big blue-green eyes."

Despite her resolve to act sophisticated and mature on the phone, she giggled like a love-struck high schooler. The very sound of his sexy voice was honestly giving her the shivers.

"Listen, Jess, back to the favor. I know it's shamefully short notice and all, but I was wondering if you'd like to attend the IM Awards gala with me Friday night?"

Jessica's pulse increased to hummingbird speed. One of her lifelong dreams was to attend the IM Awards gala! She'd been born craving the excitement of Hollywood. Now it was being laid at her feet. Friday night she could be right in the middle of it all: spotlights, flashbulbs, applauding fans, shoulder-to-shoulder celebrities parading down the red carpet. . . .

"Jessica?" Charles's voice broke into her daydream. "How about it?"

She opened her mouth to say yes, but Charles had to go and spoil everything.

". . . I was planning on taking Maria Margoletti," he continued. "But the movie she's working on is way over schedule. She'll be stuck on location in France for at least another three weeks."

Jessica clamped her mouth shut with a huff.

She hated the idea of being second choice—even to the gorgeous, exotic Maria Margoletti. Movie magazines called Maria box-office magic. Jessica called her overexposed. OK, maybe she had legs up to her armpits and a mane of glossy black curls, but that didn't mean she had acting talent. The nerve of him!

"*This* Friday?" she asked skeptically. "That *is* awfully short notice."

"If you already have plans, I'll understand." He sounded totally disappointed. "I guess I can always go with my sister and her fiancé."

"Let me check my calendar," Jessica said hurriedly before Charles gave up completely. Although jealously still prickled up and down her spine, she couldn't let an opportunity like this slip away. She *did* want to go. She flipped a few pages on a nearby magazine, pretending to check her calendar.

"Come on, Jessica. You can't let me down. I'm up for two awards. Don't you think it'd look a lot better if I had a date?"

That was better. He was beginning to sound desperate. "Oh, I imagine it would," she admitted coyly.

"Please, Jessica. Don't say no. I know it's unforgivable to ask you this late, but I only just found you again. I'm begging you."

Begging. She liked that. And as a reward she was fully prepared to forgive him—not only for

31

asking her late, but even for not asking her first. Anyway, his date with Maria had probably been nothing more than a publicity outing arranged by the movie studio.

She closed her pretend calendar noisily. "You're in luck. I don't see a single thing here that I can't rearrange—since this is a special occasion. Consider me perfectly free for the whole weekend." *And forever after that for you!* she added mentally.

"Fantastic! I'll have the limo pick you up around seven and bring you straight to my place. Then we'll ride together to the amphitheater. Oh, and after the gala there'll be at least a half-dozen obligatory parties we'll have to attend—maybe more if *Checkered Houses* wins. So don't plan on making curfew."

"No problem. I'm a big girl now. Besides, Elizabeth has been so preoccupied lately, I doubt she'll even miss me."

With Charles's warm parting of "see you soon" still ringing in her ears, Jessica tossed the cordless phone onto her bed and snatched up the *Hollywood Buzzz* magazine she'd finally found.

There was Charles's smiling face, right on the front cover. He was still every bit as handsome as she remembered. He was blessed with the same reddish brown hair and wide smile that made people call his sister, Ginger, a raving beauty. On him it looked mischievous yet sexy.

Charles Sampson! Wait till Elizabeth hears the news! she thought in excitement as she plopped back on Elizabeth's neatly made bed and closed her eyes. Why had Jessica ever thought she needed anything as idiotic as a CyberDreams Virtual Reality Fair for thrills? Her own imagination always worked just fine. She could see it now. . . .

She would be walking down the red carpet on the arm of the fabulously wealthy, famous, good-looking Charles Sampson. Throngs of people would cheer and shout praises. Cameras would flash like strobe lights from every angle. . . .

After all the publicity hoopla they'd settle into their front-row seats and watch as Ginger presented the award. Always overly dramatic, Ginger would clasp the open envelope to her breast and pause way too long. She'd let her famous smile spread from ear to ear before announcing at last, "And the Best Movie of the Year Award goes to . . . *Checkered Houses!*"

Charles would run up to that huge, glittering stage. Then with tears in his chocolaty brown eyes, he'd look out over the audience. His voice would tremble with emotion as he said, "I could never have achieved this high honor without the help of my fiancée, Jessica Wakefield. Thank you, darling. I share this night—and all nights—with you."

The camera would pan the audience and show her tearily applauding. Then it would zoom in for a close-up. There would be a collective gasp as half the eyes in the nation landed on her and saw how utterly breathtaking she looked!

"Oh no!" Jessica sat up in alarm. She leaped from the bed, her heart pounding with fright. "The IM Awards gala is *way* formal"—she flung an arm melodramatically across her forehead and fell back on the bed in an overdone swoon—"and I don't have a *single* thing to wear!"

Elizabeth stormed into her dorm room and ran straight to her desk. All the way from the quad she had been replaying her run-in with William White in her mind. And the more she thought about it, the more determined she'd become to call the police.

She reached out for the phone, but it wasn't in its usual place. She scooted a stack of art-history books to one side. Nothing. Her heart, already pounding from fear, sped up with frustration.

Elizabeth looked on the other side of her computer. Still no phone—just the answering machine and the phone's empty recharger cradle. She stared at it dumbly, as if waiting for the phone to magically reappear.

"Great!" she muttered. "The phone is gone. I'll never find it if Jessica used it last." On the verge of panic, she hit the pager button. A muffled triple beep alerted her to the phone's location.

Just as she feared, it was somewhere on Jessica's side of the room.

She turned.

Only then did she realize that she wasn't alone.

Jessica's right leg was poking out of her jam-packed closet as she stood on the toes of her left foot to reach the top shelf. Suddenly a shoe box flew from the closet and landed atop a heap of discarded clothing on the floor. Jessica, who apparently hadn't noticed Elizabeth's arrival, was muttering and mumbling as she ripped outfits off hangers and tossed them over her shoulder. Clothes were already draped over the minifridge, the vanity, and the futon. A purple halter top dangled from the lamp shade. The floor on Jessica's side of the room was calf deep in clothing, and Jessica's bed was completely buried. Still Jessica showed no signs of slowing down.

"Jessica? Um . . . what are you doing?"

Her twin glanced back at her briefly. "Have you seen that black sheath dress I wore to the Theta-Sigma formal last month?"

Elizabeth ducked as a pair of gold-lamé leggings whizzed past her head. "Jessica! Stop it. I need to talk to you."

"Maybe I loaned it to Isabella . . . or was it hers and I gave it back?" Jessica wrinkled her forehead in concentration and paused from her clothing toss for a moment. "No. I think it belonged to Lila, and maybe I—"

"It *was* Lila's," Elizabeth interjected, "but Jess—"

"*Or* . . . what about that scarlet slip dress I wore that time I had dinner at Marvioso with Bobby Hornet? Remember?" Jessica paused long enough to bite a fingernail.

"That was Lila's too, but—"

"Aw, it was too short anyway." Jessica turned back toward her closet. "I need something long. And slinky. Really, really sexy. Didn't I have a chartreuse—"

Exasperated, Elizabeth grabbed her twin's shoulder and spun her around. "Jessica Wakefield, listen to me!"

"What's up with you?" Jessica asked, her eyes growing wide.

"I just saw William White out on the quad. That's what!"

Jessica had already squirmed out of Elizabeth's grasp and was headed back for another dress. She froze midgrab and let a fluff of tangerine chiffon float to her feet. "No way. That psycho is dead! You must have been seeing things."

"Jess, I not only saw him, I talked to him. I'm one hundred percent positive he's not dead. He's very much alive and worse . . . he's right here on campus."

Jessica went pale and scrambled to Elizabeth's side. "Well, what are you waiting for? Call the police!"

"That's exactly what I was going to do *if* I could find the phone!"

Jessica hoisted an armload of clothes from her bed and dumped them onto her desk chair. Then she began scooping the remaining layers to the floor until she uncovered the phone. She shoved it into Elizabeth's hand. "Here! Call!"

With trembling fingers Elizabeth dialed the police station.

"Sweet Valley precinct. How may I direct your call?"

"May I speak to Detective Bart Kaydon, please?" she asked. "Tell him Elizabeth Wakefield is calling, and it's important."

Detective Kaydon had handled the investigation of the wreck that had supposedly killed William. He'd been the person who'd finally gathered the evidence that proved William had tried to kill Elizabeth's closest friends by cutting the brake lines on their rented van. By asking for him Elizabeth hoped to avoid rehashing memories that were better left forgotten.

It seemed like forever before she heard his gruff, scratchy voice come on the line. "Detective Kaydon here. How can I help you, Miss Wakefield? The officer who answered the phone said you sounded upset."

"Yes, I am upset. And I have every reason to be. You're probably not going to believe this, but William White is still alive!"

She half hoped Detective Kaydon would argue with her—convince her that she was imagining things, but he sighed tiredly. "I'd hoped you'd never find out."

This was not the answer she expected. "You mean you *knew* he was alive all this time and never told me?" She swallowed loudly. "I think you owe me an explanation."

Elizabeth heard papers rattling. Evidently Detective Kaydon had opened William's file and spread it on his desk while she was talking. No doubt it was a very *thick* file since it took the detective a long time to speak again.

"William White didn't die in that wreck, Miss Wakefield. His condition was touch and go for a while, but he survived. . . ."

Elizabeth almost dropped the phone.

"While still in the hospital, he gave himself up to the police. As soon as his condition was stable, he was moved to the prison hospital."

Elizabeth switched the phone to her other hand and wiped her sweaty palm on her jeans. "You *knew* this? And you let me go on believing he was dead?" She grabbed the corner of her desk for support. "You let me go on thinking I'd . . . I'd *killed* him? Why didn't anyone tell me he was alive?"

Detective Kaydon cleared his throat. "We knew how traumatized you were by this guy. We thought it would be better to leave you in the dark."

"You didn't just leave me in the dark. You deceived me!"

"No one tried to—"

"No? What would you call it?" She edged away from Jessica, who was trying to listen in on the conversation. "Everyone told me William was dead," she continued. "The White family's lawyer came to see me. I actually inherited William's trust fund. If William wasn't dead, why would his family give me his inheritance? I didn't ask for his money. I didn't even want it. I gave away every penny of it to charity, except for enough to take my friends on a cruise. I figured they deserved it . . . after nearly being killed."

"Who knows? Maybe the family let you have the money for the same reason . . . they felt you deserved it after all you'd been through."

"What I *deserve* is a feeling of security in my own life." Elizabeth paused long enough to wave Jessica out of her face again. "Were you also aware that William is no longer in your prison hospital?"

"Of course."

"Of course?" Elizabeth repeated incredulously. Her temperature rose several degrees. "You sound like you're reading the day's weather report. How can you sit there so nonchalantly and tell me you know a criminally insane lunatic has escaped? Do you guys let this happen every day?"

"William hasn't escaped. He was released."

"*Released*? No way!" Elizabeth's knees would no longer support her weight. She sank down onto the edge of her bed.

Jessica plopped down beside her, motioning that she wanted to be filled in on what Detective Kaydon was saying. Elizabeth leaned away and put her hand over her exposed ear to cut off the sound of Jessica's whispers. She heard more papers being shuffled on Detective Kaydon's end of the line.

"Hmmm—White was released to the care of his psychiatrist, Dr. Orrin Denby."

"That's insane! What were you people thinking?"

Detective Kaydon's voice rose slightly. "You know very well that California prisons are impossibly overcrowded. Our penal health facilities are overloaded beyond belief. We're not about to squabble if some rich, do-gooder psychiatrist offers to take a nutcase off our hands. Saves the taxpayers a lot of money."

"I see." Elizabeth stood, her terror turning to indignation. "So you're willing to have dead bodies scattered all over southern California as long as the taxpayers are saved a few dollars?"

"Elizabeth, I don't know where you got your news, and I can understand that you are upset to find out White is still alive, but you can rest easy. You're perfectly safe, and so are all the other residents of southern California—at least as far as

William White is concerned. Dr. Denby has the guy sedated and locked safely away."

"Locked away? Then how can you explain why I saw William White today—right here on the SVU campus?"

There was a noticeable pause before Detective Kaydon answered. "My guess would be that you've let the news of White's return to the living scare you into imagining things."

Elizabeth's voice rose to an uncomfortable pitch. "I didn't *imagine* anything. I talked to him. Face-to-face. He's here, following me. Scaring me just like before."

"That's impossible."

"I'm telling you what I saw—"

"And I'm telling you what you *didn't* see. You *didn't* see the shape White was in after that car wreck. You didn't see him lying there trussed up like a mummy in that hospital bed, and you didn't see him being taken away to Denby's clinic, propped in a wheelchair like a drooling lump of Play-Doh. The poor guy's face hit the windshield of that car hard enough to shatter it. And if that wasn't enough, he got toasted by a fire that started before we could get him free. William White is practically a turnip. There's no way you could have seen him on your campus! Now if you'll excuse me, I don't have time for dealing with coed hysterics."

Elizabeth threw the phone across the room.

"What did he say?" Jessica asked, hovering over her shoulder. "What's going on?"

Jessica had tried to follow Elizabeth's ranting explanation, but the way her sister kept pacing up and down the room, sitting down, then jumping up, made Jessica dizzy. All she wanted to know was if the cops were going to come lock up that kook William White. She didn't have time for all the boring details. Losing her patience, she grabbed Elizabeth and wrestled her into her desk chair.

"OK. Slow down and explain to me calmly. Is Detective Kaydon sending someone over here or not?"

"Not!" Elizabeth popped back up like a jack-in-the-box.

"Why not? Didn't he believe you?"

Elizabeth shook her head so hard, her ponytail loosened. "He said I couldn't possibly have seen William because he's locked away under the care of some world-famous psychiatrist named Dr. Denby."

Jessica let out a sigh of relief. Elizabeth had her half worried to death—all for nothing. "That's great news. Even if William isn't dead, like we thought, he can't hurt you if he's in a nuthouse."

"Detective Kaydon also said that William is practically a vegetable."

"All the better. You're safe. So why can't you let it go?"

"Because Detective Kaydon is wrong. The guy I saw out on the quad was definitely William White the Second. And he was no vegetable. He had some . . . scars, but he looked as healthy as he ever did."

"Are you *sure* it was William?" She was beginning to believe her sister was imagining things.

"Jessica!"

"OK, OK, I believe you," Jessica said, putting up her hands in a defensive gesture. "So, maybe he's cured."

"Cured from being a vegetable or cured from being insane?" Elizabeth sneered.

"Both." Jessica shrugged. "Well, don't look at me like I'm crazy. It's possible, isn't it? I'm sure this Dr. Dumby knows what he's doing."

"Denby."

"Whatever. But anyway, he's bound to be good, or else the cops wouldn't have released William to him. And if he's good, then surely he wouldn't allow William to roam around free on campus unless he's cured. Forget about it."

"But Jess, I can't just forget about him. He tried to kill me . . . and Tom and Isabella and Nina . . . and Bryan and even Celine. . . ."

Jessica's interest in Elizabeth's false alarm was waning fast. Elizabeth always overreacted. Besides, her closet was calling to her. "I know, he tried to kill *everybody*," she said impatiently. "But you worry too much. You know the cops would come on the double if there was any chance you were in danger. We've just got to assume William is cured and not let him bother us anymore."

"I can't accept that. Just because he says he's changed and some psychiatrist says he's changed—"

"Will you listen to yourself? I can't believe this; Miss Help-the-Misunderstood Wakefield not giving someone a second chance? Aren't you the one who's always preaching about getting to know someone before judging them? Sheesh!"

"But what if he starts with the notes and—"

"He hasn't done anything like that yet, has he?"

"No, but today he . . . he gave me a rose."

"Big scare! C'mon, Elizabeth, there's no crime in handing out flowers. Most women would love getting roses. I know I would."

"Not from a psychotic murderer!"

"Hey, roses are roses."

Elizabeth stomped her foot. "Don't joke! This is serious!"

"Oh, get a grip. I'm just being logical. William *has* to be cured, or he wouldn't be free. I'm sure he's completely changed."

"That's exactly what he claimed."

"Then there you go. Case closed." Jessica walked back to her closet and began searching for the perfect dress.

"Jess, there's more."

"What?" she asked impatiently over her shoulder.

"Today isn't the first time I've seen William. I mean, it's the first time I've seen the *real* William, but . . . I've been seeing William all week in that virtual-reality tent."

"Your CyberDream fantasies were about William White? I thought you said you were dreaming of vast, endless, boring libraries."

"Yes. But I didn't mention that William was chasing me through those libraries."

"No wonder you've been so bummed all week."

Elizabeth looked down at her feet. "Do you think I wanted to see William?"

"Of course not! It was just some warped nightmare."

"But Jonah Falk said we'd live out our most desired fantasies. Do you think it's possible that I have some sort of sick attraction to William White?"

"No! I mean . . . well . . . you *did* think he was Mr. Perfect once."

"I know. But it was right after Todd and I broke up, and I was so hurt and upset that I wasn't seeing clearly. Why else would I have been gullible enough to think that he was the answer to all my problems?"

"Maybe because he was polite, polished, rich, sophisticated, and hotter than a male model on a good day."

"But don't you see? He wasn't what he seemed

45

then, so why couldn't he be pretending to be cured now? You don't know what a good actor William is."

Jessica was insulted. She knew more about acting than Elizabeth ever would. She was practically an actress herself. "I don't think he could fool a psychiatrist, Liz."

"He has before."

Jessica threw up her hands and rolled her eyes. "Well, if this Dr. Denby is so good, he won't be fooled." She was tired of talking about creepy old William White. Turning back to her closet, she pulled out a royal blue, knit tube dress, held it in front of her, and moved to the mirror.

"What if he starts harassing me again?"

"Then we'll call campus security or the police and have his preppy butt thrown back in jail, that's what!" Annoyed at her sister's self-absorption, Jessica threw the blue dress onto the discard pile. "Jeez! It's almost two, and I still don't have a clue about what to wear."

"Two?" Elizabeth whirled around and checked her alarm clock as if she didn't trust Jessica to tell time. "I'm supposed to be at the library right now. I totally forgot that the archives committee was supposed to meet at one-thirty." She grabbed a hairbrush and began to repair her drooping ponytail.

Jessica sighed. Now maybe things could get back to normal.

Suddenly a loud knock sounded at the door. Elizabeth's brush went flying as she squealed in fright.

"Who's that?" she cried, dashing across the room. She grabbed Jessica's arm. "What if it's Will—"

Jessica cried out and peeled away her sister's vise grip. "Yow, you *really* know how to spoil someone's good mood."

Angrily Jessica stomped across the room and jerked open the door.

"Jessica, no! Don't open the door! It could be—"

Chapter Three

"Oh, it's *you*," Jessica said in a bored tone.

"Nice to see you too, Jessica," Tom replied. He wasn't in the mood to trade insults. He stepped around Jessica and quickly scanned the room for Elizabeth. He felt as if he were witnessing the aftermath of an explosion in a clothing factory. "What's going on, Jess? Did your closet finally burst at the seams?"

"Ha-ha, very funny." She harrumphed and flounced over to her closet, where she began flinging clothes around as if she were racing to empty it out.

Tom looked over at Elizabeth. With her wide, blue-green eyes and little tendrils of hair falling around her face, she was as lovely as ever. Maybe a tad too much blush for her pale complexion, but she didn't seem to be in any imminent danger. He must have dreamed the whole fleeing-in-terror episode.

As he moved farther into the room, she seemed to stiffen. On second glance, maybe she *did* look a little bit upset. But knowing her, she was probably mad at Jessica for the mess.

He smiled, proud of his intuitiveness. The nerve of Jonah Falk, insinuating that Tom didn't understand Elizabeth. He could read her like a Teleprompter. Although Elizabeth and Jessica were closer than any two people he'd ever known, they did occasionally have differences of opinion—sometimes rather loud ones. More than likely, he'd just walked in on another of their sisterly snits.

Relieved, he sat down on Elizabeth's bed and cradled his head in his hands. After sprinting all the way to Dickenson Hall, his head was throbbing so badly, he thought it might split wide open. "What a morning," he groaned. He looked up at Elizabeth, expecting a bit of sympathy. When she didn't respond, he tried again. "I've got the headache to end all headaches."

Elizabeth still made no response. She just stood towering over him like some annoyed sentry. Her arms were folded across her chest, shutting him out.

A white silk blouse flew in front of Tom's face and landed on the floor. "What the—"

Elizabeth leaned over, picked up the blouse, folded it neatly, and laid it on the bed beside Tom.

"What's with her?" he asked, nodding toward Jessica.

Elizabeth shrugged. "She's been like this ever since I got home."

Tom returned her shrug. "Typical Jessica." He patted the bed beside him and then held out his arm to her. "Sit down here and let me tell you about the crummy day I've had. I could use a little TLC right now."

Elizabeth stepped away, and Tom let his arm fall limply to his side. *What's her deal?* he wondered. He'd worried himself half sick about her, and now that he expected a little sympathy in return, she was acting like an icicle. It seemed as if they'd done nothing but fight lately—all because of that virtual-reality mess. He'd be glad when things got back to normal.

"So what are we going to do this afternoon?" he asked, hoping to break through her mood.

A crash came from Jessica's side of the room. A pair of platform shoes had come flying out of her closet. They'd hit the metal wastebasket, overturning it.

Tom grabbed his head as the noise rattled in his ears. "Something *quiet*, I hope," he whispered hoarsely.

"Actually, I was just on my way out," Elizabeth said.

"Oh, come on, I don't want to go out. I was hoping we could just laze around the rest of the afternoon. I've got a crease in the back of my head the size of the San Andreas Fault, and—"

"I said *I* was on my way out. You can stay here if you want, but I'm headed for the library."

"Hey." He reached for her arm again. "You can go to the library anytime. Why don't we rent a video—one of those old black-and-white movies you like—and go back to my room and—"

"Tom, you aren't listening to me—as usual."

"Huh? What were you saying?"

"I said, I have a meeting at the library. I'm already late."

Tom glowered. "What kind of meeting?"

"The archive thing."

"*What* archive thing?"

Her glare was so harsh, Tom actually winced. "I told you about it last week."

Tom shook his head, immediately regretting the movement. "Maybe you only thought you told me. If it is all that important, I'm sure I'd have remembered."

Her bright eyes glazed over with annoyance.

He shrugged. "OK, then. Refresh my memory. What's the archive thing?"

She sighed in a way that always irked him. "For WSVU's number-one star news reporter, you sure don't keep up much, do you?" she said sarcastically. "Oh yeah, I forgot. You've been too busy slaying dragons and rescuing princesses."

It *was* still the virtual-reality thing! He should have known.

"Well, for your information," she continued,

"when that leak in the library's basement was getting repaired, a concrete wall broke away, and it revealed this door that led to a whole network of tunnels and passages under the library. They're some kind of archives. I'm on the committee that's going to explore the place and catalog what we find down there."

"Aw, ditch it. Leave it for the history nuts."

"I can't. I promised I'd help. Besides, I *want* to do it. This could be really exciting."

"Why are you always volunteering for stuff when you barely have time for me as it is?"

Elizabeth's hands flew to her hips. "Tom, why is everything always about *you*? I have a life too, you know."

"I didn't mean it that way." A bright paisley scarf landed on Tom's head and he angrily snatched it away. He turned and glared at Jessica's back.

"Then exactly how did you mean it?"

Tom turned back to Elizabeth. "I'm just saying, a girl should make a little time for her boyfriend somewhere in the day. Why else bother?"

"Hmmm. Good point," Elizabeth said, snatching up her leather backpack. "Why bother at all? This *girl* is leaving."

"Wait! I'm not through—"

"But *I* am." Elizabeth threw her backpack over one shoulder and moved to the door.

Tom rose to catch her arm, but just as he

reached out, Jessica stepped into his path.

"Now, where's that silk blouse?" she muttered. "I know I had it just a second ago." Jessica bent over right in front of him and rummaged through a pile of clothes.

Tom dodged to one side, but Jessica blocked him again. He was beginning to feel as if he were back on the football field. Feigning a move to the left, he slipped around her on the right, but he was too late. Elizabeth was out the door and down the hall before he had a chance. There was no way he could catch her now—not the way he felt. Tom dropped back onto Elizabeth's bed and cradled his pounding head in his hands.

"There it is! *Tom,* you're *sitting* on it!" Jessica shrieked. She began pushing against his thigh with one hand and tugging on the sleeve of a white blouse with the other.

"Can I help you with something?" Tom snapped.

Jessica yanked once more. The sleeve came away in her hand. Glaring, she whacked him over the head with the scrap of silk. "Not unless you have a formal gown I could borrow!"

Elizabeth ducked her head and followed John Petrie, the head archives librarian, through a gaping hole in the concrete wall at one end of the library's basement. She sneezed as concrete dust and the musky odor of damp earth filled her nose.

"Gesundheit!" John called over his shoulder.

"Thanks," Elizabeth said with a sniff. She followed him down three steep stone steps and through an arched doorway into the narrow, tunnel-like passage that led to the archives. Overhead, a makeshift lighting system had been rigged up; dozens of extension cords had been connected end to end. Although a bare bulb dangled every eight or ten feet, the passage was still dark and gloomy. But Elizabeth didn't mind. She was thrilled to be one of the few students included in this very important project.

"This is so exciting!" she said. "I feel just like an archaeologist."

"It's incredible," John agreed. "Just imagine, all these rooms and passages have sat beneath our library undisturbed for nearly a hundred years. It's like we've cracked open a time capsule."

"Or a tomb." Elizabeth shivered. The farther they went, the creepier the place seemed. She almost expected to turn the corner and see hieroglyphics on the wall.

As the floor sloped downward at a sharp angle for several yards, Elizabeth slowed her pace. She had to concentrate on her feet to keep from stumbling ahead and into John.

"I wonder why this place was sealed off?" she asked when the floor leveled off again.

John shrugged his skinny shoulders. "Accident would be my guess. Some lazy work detail probably thought a solid concrete wall would be easier to build than a doorway. One summer, back when I was working my way through college doing construction . . ."

Elizabeth suppressed a giggle. John's story was totally lost on her as she tried to imagine him doing any sort of construction work. He looked like Ichabod Crane from *The Legend of Sleepy Hollow*—Disney's cartoon version. He was a tall, almost skeletal man, all arms, legs, feet, and elbows. She couldn't imagine him lifting a hammer without keeling over.

They turned to the left and stepped into another dank passageway with a ceiling so low, Elizabeth could feel her hair being ruffled as they walked. John, considerably taller than her five-foot six, had to walk hunched over with his head crooked to one side. They made yet another sharp turn. The next hallway they entered seemed less claustrophobic, thanks to a higher ceiling and openings off each side. Elizabeth peeked into a couple of the openings. Each led to a small, dark room.

"This is unbelievable. All this turning and twisting; it's like a maze," Elizabeth commented.

"It's even worse than you can imagine. Every day that we've worked down here, we've discovered a new room or passageway. There's no telling how many more nooks and crannies are waiting to be found."

"I hope I can find my way back out of here

again. Maybe I should have dropped bread crumbs or something to leave a trail."

John gasped and threw out his skinny arms, bringing them both to a halt. "No—you mustn't bring food into the archives— not ever! We don't know if there are rats or bats or what living down here, but every once in a while we've smelled . . . something. We can't take the risk of attracting vermin."

"I meant that as a joke, John."

"Oh yeah. Of course it was. I get it." He made a nasal noise that passed for a laugh, then abruptly stopped with a snort. "But seriously, don't bring any food down here."

"I won't." She smothered a grin. "I'll use a string to guide me out."

"You won't need it. If you do happen to get turned around, all you have to do is follow the light cords."

"Thanks. I'll keep that in mind." Evidently there was no use in trying to kid around with John. He was a serious librarian through and through.

"Why do you think all these secret tunnels were built in the first place?" she asked.

He raised his arms in something resembling a shrug. The crook of his bony elbows made him look like a big *W*. "Nobody knows for sure, but there are several theories. We're hoping to find something down here that will give us some definite answers as to the history of the place. Like yesterday, we found a large room full of old wooden wine kegs. So I think maybe the property adjacent to the original library was a winery at one time and this was the wine cellar."

"I guess with all the additions and remodeling over the years, it makes sense. We aren't all that far from wine country."

"You know Professor Spicer? With the religious history department? He claims that we're bound to find a room full of bibles and religious tracts down here somewhere. He believes this was once part of a Spanish monastery. It's possible, I guess. There were a lot of Spanish missions and Franciscan monasteries in this part of the state back in the eighteenth and nineteenth centuries. If Spicer's theory is correct, then these passages could even be older than we think."

Elizabeth was about to ask him how much farther they had to go when he stopped in front of an arched opening in the wall and threw out his arms. "Here we are," he announced grandly.

As Elizabeth stepped forward to see, her foot caught on something. She stumbled into John, sending him bouncing into the wall.

His friendliness suddenly disappeared. "Be careful," he growled.

The light was so dim, she had to bend down to see what had tripped her. "What *is* that?" she asked, pointing to a strange-looking pipe that stuck out from the doorway about eight inches. It was as black as a cast-iron skillet and had a weird-looking nozzle on the end.

"That's an ancient natural-gas pipe. Probably here for gas lighting long ago, or maybe heat."

Elizabeth reached out with her foot and nudged it.

"Be careful, will you? The last thing we need down here is a gas leak. Natural gas can be dangerous. Not only is it deadly to breathe, but it can be extremely explosive."

"You don't think it's still hooked up, do you?"

"I'm sure it is. But we haven't found the source yet. Dr. Johansen from the geology department claims it might even come from a direct pocket of natural gas beneath the campus. So watch it. We don't want you to blow us sky-high, do we?"

"No, we wouldn't want that."

He craned his neck around and poked his long nose right in her face. "That was a joke, Elizabeth."

She suddenly began to laugh. Not because of John's lame joke, but because the guy was so out of it.

His Adam's apple bobbed up and down and he gave her a goofy, lopsided grin. "I like you, Elizabeth," he said, as if he were bestowing her with a great honor. "Not everyone understands my humor the way you do. I think it may be a bit dry for the younger generation."

Elizabeth bit her bottom lip and took a deep

breath to control her giggles. "Maybe a bit," she agreed.

"Well, this is the end of the line," he said, waving grandly. "Come on in here and get to work."

Watching out for any additional protruding pipes, Elizabeth eased inside. The wall opposite the door was lined with ceiling-to-floor bookshelves. Although they were covered with dust and cobwebs, she could tell the wood was dark and heavy. The books were very, very old. The gigantic rolltop desk on the right side of the room looked like a prop from a cowboy movie. Every frontier bank must have had one just like it. She crossed over to it and slid open the dusty top.

"A-a-a-choo!"

"You might want to wait a few days before starting if you're coming down with a cold," John advised.

"It's just the dust." She pulled a tissue from her pocket. "I feel fine."

John walked over to the left side of the room and reached to the top of one of the three large, wooden file cabinets. "This is some kind of records room, and for all we know, it may be the key to the whole mystery. Your job is to go through every drawer of these file cabinets and catalog the contents." He handed her a clipboard and tapped a bony finger on the top page. "We've assigned numbers to each file cabinet and letters of the alphabet to each drawer. Be sure and list everything exactly in the order and location you find it. Include any pertinent dates and descriptions. They may be important later."

Elizabeth took the clipboard and nodded. She wondered how she was going to read his scratchy handwriting in the dim light of the single bulb that hung just inside the open doorway.

"Oh, and when you leave, don't worry—just follow the light cords. But try not to yank on them. If one comes unplugged, every light beyond that spot will go out."

That didn't sound very reassuring.

When John disappeared back into the gloomy passageway, Elizabeth looked around the room almost in awe. She lovingly ran her hand along the top of the first file cabinet. As she grasped the handle and tugged, she felt like a treasure hunter. Slowly the swollen wood squeaked open to reveal a drawer that was jam-packed with yellowing, dusty-smelling file folders; each was literally crammed with papers. There was enough work here to keep her busy for the rest of the semester!

Elizabeth smiled. Maybe Tom thought her interests were time wasting and boring, but she could hardly wait to dig in and discover the past.

"Thank you, Dr. Denby. I feel so much better," William said, sitting up on the edge of the couch and running a hand through his hair.

61

"Lie back down, William. I don't think we're finished."

"I've taken too much of your time already."

"Don't block me out. This is no time to start holding back your feelings from me."

William glanced guiltily in Dr. Denby's direction, but he couldn't meet his gaze. "I'm not."

"I can feel you shutting doors between us." Dr. Denby made a clucking sound with his tongue. "All the progress we've made has been because we've had an honest, open relationship. I thought you trusted me."

"I do trust you—more than I've ever trusted anyone."

"Then what is it?" Dr. Denby demanded relentlessly. "What is the secret that you're trying to keep from me?"

"Nothing," William insisted. "I've been honest with you from the start. You know every awful thing I've ever done. You know every dark thought I've ever had."

"You can only be free of your demons when you unburden your heart. Redemption is yours, but only if you cooperate."

"I *am* cooperating. Completely. You know I am." William gnawed on a fingernail. Sometimes the man was simply too insightful.

"Tell me, William. What is weighing on your soul?"

Dr. Denby's nagging was wearing him down.

"It's Elizabeth!" he finally blurted. He crossed his arms tightly over his heart.

"There must be something more on your mind. We've been talking about Elizabeth's forgiveness for an hour."

"I want more from her than just forgiveness. I want her love." Although he knew Dr. Denby preferred him to stay on the couch, William couldn't contain his nervous energy. He jumped up and began to pace around the room. "I love her. I've always loved her. Never has there been a more perfect woman for me. She's not only beautiful—she's brilliant and kindhearted. She reads Shakespeare and listens to classical music. She makes me smile. From the very first moment I saw her at that Sigma party, way back when she first came to the university, I knew that she was my soul mate, even though she *was* associating with those . . . inferior people. It didn't matter to me who her friends were or who her family was. Nothing mattered except . . . I knew I had to have her. From that night on, I haven't even thought about another woman." He hurried over to Dr. Denby's side. "How could I? What other woman could ever hope to live up to my perfect Elizabeth?"

"But you tried to kill her."

William sighed. Why did Dr. Denby have to constantly remind him of his mistakes? "I was confused and lost because she said she didn't love me. But I never meant to hurt her. Never! Even when

I was angry with her, I still loved her." William dropped back onto the couch and lowered his head. Depression swelled up inside him, filling his chest with a pain so real, he could almost touch it.

"Stay with me, William. Don't give in to these dark thoughts."

"How can I win her heart, Dr. Denby? Even if she can look past my scars, can she ever look past the horrible things I did to her and her friends?"

"Past all. All is past. Now you must show Elizabeth that you are a new person. You've been reborn, heart and soul."

"But *how* can I show her?"

"That you must discover for yourself."

"But if I lose her——"

"You won't. Not if you walk the path of true love and follow your heart—your *new* heart."

"I'll try," William said weakly. But looking into Dr. Denby's stern, serious face steeled his courage. If Dr. Denby had faith in him, why shouldn't he have faith in himself? He straightened his shoulders and took a deep breath. "I *swear* I will try," William vowed.

Chapter Four

Tom stared up at the pitch-black ceiling of studio number one with its jumble of lights, catwalks, and wires but saw nothing. His body had made it to work, but his mind was still across campus—in room 28, Dickenson Hall. Elizabeth's room. He'd been sitting in the deserted studio, staring into the darkness for fifteen minutes, trying to picture Elizabeth's face. It was the weirdest thing; no matter how hard he tried, he couldn't do it.

It wasn't that he'd forgotten what she looked like. It was just that he couldn't bring her image to mind the way he once could. He fed himself the facts: blond hair, aqua eyes, heart-shaped face, adorable dimple, but none of it was coming together. Again he blamed the virtual-reality dreams. They had him spooked.

I do know Elizabeth! he assured himself. *I know her better than . . . no, apparently I don't.* He sighed loudly. Things were changing between them, and he didn't know what to do. Not only was Elizabeth not the perfect princess of his CyberDream, but she was no longer the perfect girl he'd met at that Sigma party at the beginning of the year. Practically overnight she'd become self-centered and short-tempered. Worst of all, she never had time for him anymore.

He thought back to that party. The moment he had walked into Sigma house and had seen her across the room, he'd known she was the only woman he'd ever love. She was beautiful, but that was a given. There'd been something else, some indescribable quality about her, that made him feel they were soul mates from their very first hello. They were so alike. Sure enough, he soon found out she hated frat parties as much as he did. They were both attending the Sigma party only to humor friends. They both wanted to be investigative reporters and cared about correcting social injustices. And they were both looking for an honest, caring relationship.

They hadn't immediately fallen into each other's arms—as much as Tom would have liked to. It took them what felt like ages to get to know each other, trust each other, and love each other. But as far as Tom was concerned, the delay was for Elizabeth's benefit. He knew from the start that she was the one.

"Earth to Tom."

Startled, Tom looked down to see freckle-faced Julie Fiore, the most recent addition to the WSVU staff, waving a chubby arm in front of his face. "What?"

"Did you hear a word I just said?" she asked.

"No." He shook his head apologetically. "I'm afraid I didn't. Not until the 'Earth to Tom' part."

"Do I have enough of your attention to try again?" She rolled her eyes in mock annoyance, but her giggle gave away her true feelings.

He couldn't help but smile back. Julie was one of the most cheerful people he'd ever met. She seemed to spread sunshine inside the TV studio. Maybe that was why Professor Sedder had sent her over. WSVU had certainly not been the happiest of workplaces lately. *Thanks mainly to the gloomy mood of its manager—me,* Tom thought guiltily.

Julie didn't get the job because of her skills, that was for sure. Although she seemed to be catching on fast, she knew absolutely nothing about working in television journalism when she first started at WSVU. But maybe Tom wasn't being fair. Like everything else he did, even his judgment at work was being affected by thoughts of Elizabeth. Maybe he judged Julie too harshly simply because he still missed Elizabeth's presence at the station. Ever since she'd gone over to the *Sweet Valley Gazette* and begun working her way up through the ranks of the campus newspaper, Tom had felt shorthanded around the TV station.

No one had been able to live up to Elizabeth's legacy of efficiency and dedication.

"Tom?" Julie nudged gently against his arm. "I asked if you wanted to use the library-archives story for the afternoon news broadcast."

Tom crashed back to earth. "No," he growled.

"But it should be a good story. They're finding all kinds of historical items in those rooms below the library's basement. There are all these tunnels—"

"I know," he interrupted, hoping to tone down his earlier gruffness. "We'll do the story eventually, but I want to hold off on it for now. I, uh, still have a few more facts to check."

"OK." She checked her clipboard. "Oh, and Professor Sedder called. He said to let you know that your requisition for the new computer that'll link us to the weather station has been approved."

"What?" Tom blinked. "I'm sorry. Who did you say?"

"Who else approves requisitions? Professor Sedder, the faculty adviser."

"And what did he approve?"

"OK." Julie placed her hands on her ample hips. "Give it up. Talk to Julie. What's got you so frazzled? It can't be work because you haven't been here enough over the past three days to let that affect you. I should know; I'm the flunky who's had to take all your messages. Where have you been anyway?"

"Busy," he muttered. He was too ashamed to admit he'd been hanging around that CyberDreams tent, wasting his time living fantasies that had no hope of ever becoming real. Not that he really wanted them to . . . not after the way they ended.

"And I know you don't have classes on your mind because you have two messages here from your roommate, Danny Wyatt, wanting to know why you cut econ and advanced communications."

Tom winced. He had been neglecting everything lately.

"That leaves only one thing," Julie continued. "Problems with your love life."

Tom felt himself blushing, but Julie continued without the least hint of embarrassment.

"It's OK. You can tell Julie. They don't call me Dr. Heartache for nothing. All my friends come to me with their problems. As many times as I've been dumped on, I practically have a degree in makeups and breakups. I could probably write a dating-advice column for the *Gazette*."

Tom wasn't interested in losing any more employees to the school newspaper—not even in joking about it. "Don't be talking about the *Gazette*, traitor. Try to remember, you're in TV journalism now."

"Hey, that's right! I could have my own talk show here at WSVU. No nuts or sluts, though—

strictly love problems and solutions. I love it! Want me to audition?" She set down her clipboard and stuck her pencil behind her ear. "We could start with fifteen minutes right between the news and the weekly calendar. At least until my popularity soars and the switchboard gets overloaded with calls for me. Then you'll be forced to give me a bigger spot. Maybe the hour allotted for the nightly campus news, whaddaya say?"

Tom grinned sheepishly. "Are you ever serious?"

She swiped her hand across her face and pretended to wipe her smile into an exaggerated frown. "OK, this is my serious business face. No more kidding around," she said in an unnaturally deep voice. "Why don't you tell Dr. Heartache what's really bugging you?"

"Well, Dr. Heartbreak—"

"—ache!"

"I *am* aching! And I'm tired of being ignored. How can I get my girlfriend to pay more attention to me?"

Julie scurried over to the news anchor's desk and plopped into the chair. She folded her pudgy arms in front of her, stared into the nearest camera, and cleared her throat noisily. "Good morning, my lovesick viewers. Today's answer is for 'Ignored and Distracted.' The solution to your problem is simple. If you want your girlfriend to pay more attention to you, then you obviously need to pay more attention to *her*. Show her you still love her. Maybe she's forgotten what it was like in the beginning of your relationship when your love was fresh and exciting."

Grinning despite his misery, Tom walked over to the news desk. He rested his elbows opposite Julie, leaned close, and whispered confidentially, "But Dr. Heartache, that's easier said than done. How can I show her I still love her as much as I did the first time I saw her . . . maybe even more, if that's possible?"

"Say it with flowers."

Tom wrinkled his nose and backed away. "Just flowers? Isn't that a bit clichéd?"

"Hey, you get what you pay for, buddy. Free advice is free advice." Julie winked and laughed. "But seriously, try the flowers. It's a classic, not a cliché."

Tom looked at her skeptically.

"Trust me. If we're talking about that cute little blonde whose picture is so prominently displayed on the desk in your office, I'd say she's a classics kind of girl."

"Maybe you're right."

"Of course I am. Dr. Heartache knows whereof she speaks. And remember, sometimes the classics are classics for a reason. They work. Try it. I give you my money-back guarantee."

Flowers, Tom thought. Why not? He'd tried everything else. Besides, he had nothing left to lose.

*   *   *

A icy blast of air-conditioned air hit Elizabeth as the library's automatic doors swooshed open to admit her. It seemed as if she'd just left and now here she was, back again.

She hurried over to the computerized catalog to check the availability of research material on Shakespeare. Her English-lit paper wasn't due for another three weeks, but with so much reading to do, she couldn't save everything for the last minute—especially now that she had so much work to do in the archives.

Finding the information she needed, she reached for a slip of paper, pulled a pencil from her backpack, and jotted down the call numbers of three books.

"Hey, Liz!" John Petrie leaned over the counter beside her.

"Hi, John. You're working late."

"I was about to say the same thing to you. I'd think you'd have had enough of the library."

"You sound like my boyfriend," she muttered, rolling her eyes.

"You're not cataloging tonight, are you?"

"Nope." She held up the scrap of paper. "Research paper. Shakespeare."

"Can I help you with anything?"

She groaned as she lifted her backpack to her shoulder. "Not unless you can tell me why the heaviest books are always on the third floor."

"Actually, they're not."

Elizabeth smiled. She'd momentarily forgotten

John's inability to joke. "I didn't mean it literally. That was just my silly way of complaining about having to lug a ton of books down three flights of stairs."

"I knew you were kidding," he said. "But Shakespeare isn't on the third floor."

"John, you may be a librarian, but I've spent enough time in this library to know my way around. I know where—"

"You know where Shakespeare *used* to be. Due to some bizarre leaks on the third floor, we've had to temporarily move all literary criticism books eight hundred to nine ninety-nine down to the basement stacks."

"Oh. Well, thanks for telling me."

"No problem. There's a sign upstairs, redirecting people to the basement, but I'm happy to have saved you the grueling trip up and down those stairs."

Elizabeth chuckled at John's attempt at humor, but her cheeriness didn't last long. As soon as she started down the noisy concrete stairs with their metal slip guards, she quit smiling.

Although she loved the library, the basement wasn't one of her favorite places. Sadly ignored by the recent remodeling craze on campus, it was the last holdout of slick, bare concrete floors, institutional green paint, and flickering fluorescent lights. Tonight it seemed that only two rows of the lights were working, leaving most of the basement in eerie shadows. She looked around for a switch but didn't see one. Well, no big deal. This was bright compared to the dingy archive room she'd been in all day.

Except for a couple huddled together on a Naugahyde sofa, the whole place was practically deserted. The sofa creaked, and Elizabeth jumped.

Not wanting to linger any longer than she had to, Elizabeth double-checked the call numbers on her scrap of paper and began hunting for the corresponding shelf.

"Here we go." She squinted at the row of books. The shadows between the tall shelves were so thick, it was hard to read the book titles—much less the scrawled call numbers. She browsed down the shelf until she found the first book on her list. She reached for the large volume slightly above chin level, but just as her fingers closed over the familiar cardboard spine, the book moved.

"Wha—" She jerked her fingers away and glanced nervously around. She was the only person in the narrow aisle. She reached up again. This time the book was suddenly pulled out of her grasp from the other side of the stacks.

"Elizabeth," a voice whispered.

She froze. Swallowing loudly, she stood on tiptoe and peered through the chink left by the removed book. She saw a movement—hardly more than a blur of a dark-clad shoulder. Then suddenly a bright blue eye peered back at her.

She jumped away.

"Elizabeth," the voice repeated.

Cautiously she moved back to the opening and peeked through. The person on the opposite side of the shelf backed away just enough for her to see the unscarred side of his face. "William!" she cried.

A feeling of déjà vu crept over her. She'd been here before. She'd already lived this same exact moment. Whether it'd been in real life or in her CyberDreams hardly mattered. She just knew she didn't want to be here now. She turned away from the opening and leaned the back of her head against the row of books.

"Where are you?" William whispered. "Don't run off. I've been waiting for you."

No. This couldn't be happening! She had almost convinced herself that seeing William yesterday on the quad had been a fluke—the result of an overstressed imagination. Now here he was again. Stalking her . . . again.

Once before, when William had escaped from the Harrington Institution, he had stalked her for weeks before finally making his move. What was he planning this time? She shuddered at the thought that history was about to repeat itself.

"Leave me alone!" she growled. She pulled a

book off a lower shelf and crammed it into the empty space.

"Elizabeth," he whispered again, this time appearing at the newly vacated space. "I really need to talk to you."

"William, stop it. I'm busy, and we have nothing to say to each other."

"I want you to understand what's going on with me. Won't you at least let me apologize?"

"Shhh!" The couple on the couch stared in annoyance.

Elizabeth lowered her voice. "I mean it. Leave me alone." She walked away down the stacks and busied herself by hunting for the next book on her list. When she pulled it from the shelf, there was William again.

"I don't mean to bother you or frighten you," he began, "but if you'll just hear me out—"

"No!" Elizabeth shoved the book back in place. She hurried over to the next set of shelves and reached for another book. Again William was right there waiting, whispering.

How does he do that? she wondered. No matter how fast or how quietly she moved, he was always one step ahead of her.

She tried another aisle, but it made no difference. No matter where she turned or what book she pulled off the shelf, William was right there behind it.

"Stop that!"

Grumbling and complaining, the couple gathered their belongings and left.

Now she'd done it. She'd run them off. Now she was stuck in a deserted basement—just her and William.

"I'm leaving," she declared, slamming a book back in William's face.

"You can't leave."

"I—I can't?" Elizabeth froze midstep. How did he plan to stop her? Hardly daring to breathe for fear he'd hear her, she began to tiptoe toward the end of the aisle.

She poked her head around the corner and checked to see if the coast was clear. It seemed to be. She dashed across a small, open area and around an old card catalog.

"You haven't gotten the books you came for," his voice blurted out of nowhere.

Suddenly the whole episode struck her as absurd. She leaned her forehead against the cool metal shelving of a nearby magazine rack. Her shoulders began to shake with silent laughter. William White wasn't stalking her. He was following her around like a love-starved puppy. There was nothing sinister or frightening about that. If he'd meant to hurt her, he could have jumped out and grabbed her when she first came into the basement. As dark and deserted as the place was, there was no denying he had the opportunity. She was scaring herself to death for no reason.

"William," she whispered. "Where are you?"

"Behind the magazine rack."

"Wait right there." Why not let him explain what he wanted to say? What could it hurt? Besides, she'd never get over her fears unless she faced up to them.

Suddenly William stepped from the shadows. His pale hand extended toward her, holding a long-stemmed white rose.

With a loud gasp, she slid to a stop.

"What's wrong?"

Elizabeth couldn't speak. All she could see were white roses—William's trademark. As beautiful and delicate as they were, they would forever in her mind mean a prelude to horror.

William's free hand flew up to cover his scars. "I'm so sorry. I've scared you, haven't I?" He moved forward slightly.

Elizabeth staggered back. Pity mixed with fear and shock. "N-No . . . ," she stammered. "It's . . . it's the *rose*. I hate white roses!"

William stood frozen on the edge of the shadows. But she didn't dare look into his eyes again. She would not allow herself to be moved by that pitiful, pained look.

For once she was grateful for white roses. She'd needed something to scare her to her senses. What was she thinking? After all the horrors William had subjected her to in the past, how could she have imagined him charming—even for a second?

Without another word, she turned and fled from the library.

The full moon cast quivering shadows on the sidewalk as William crept along the wall. Dressed all in black, with a black knit cap pulled low to hide his blond hair, he crouched low to keep himself hidden by the heavy shrubbery. When he reached the drooping wisteria bush, he began to count the tall, wrought-iron bars.

". . . five, six, seven, *eight!*" He grasped the eighth bar with both hands and smiled. It was still loose after all this time. With a grunt, a slight twist, and a sturdy yank, William broke the bar from the fence and let it fall noiselessly to the soft earth. Then, with a shudder, he wiped his hands on his black jeans. He'd always hated this fence, with its depressing black iron bars. *Prison bars,* he thought. All his life it seemed he'd merely passed from one prison to another. Only in the last few weeks had he known true freedom—freedom of the soul.

Remembering his mission, William slipped through the gaping hole in the fence and began to run. Except for his own breathing and the slight slapping noise his crepe-soled shoes made on the heat-softened asphalt of the winding drive, the night seemed completely soundless.

When he reached the pool area, he paused for a moment and stared back at the mansion. Its stately white brick practically glowed in the moonlight. How he wished he could think of it as a home, but he'd never been able to. It'd always been more of a museum—no, a mausoleum. Whatever, it'd never been a happy place. He stared at a single window on the second floor where the light glowed a soft yellow. Grandmother's room. How he longed to see her, to be caressed and coddled by her wrinkled hands, but it was no use going there now. William was dead to her and to all his family. They grudgingly sent money to Dr. Denby for his upkeep, but they'd made it clear long ago that he was no longer their son.

William wiped moisture from his bad eye and turned his gaze from the house to the rose garden, which stretched between the house and the pool. Nearly a half acre was filled with nothing but white benches, white paths, and the massive white roses that had once been his mother's only passion. Even though she'd been dead for a while, the flowers continued to thrive. The tall, white trellises were practically bowed under their weight.

No more roses for me, he thought. *Elizabeth and Grandmother are right. White roses are too pretentious and dramatic.* At one time he'd thought of them almost as a synonym for love. But now he knew that the white roses he'd handed around as his calling card were nothing more than a gaudy substitute for a love he was incapable of feeling—

just like his mother. That was changed now because at last he knew love—true love. He'd learned from Dr. Denby and from Elizabeth that he no longer needed the roses.

He hurried away from the pool, past the tall hedges, past the fountain. All the while keeping in the shadows. Avoiding the bright, white stone pathways, he ran all the way to the back acre of the estate. All the way to where his grandmother's rebellious response to his mother's formal rose garden lay—an open meadow sown with wildflowers.

"See this, Elizabeth?" he called to the night. "I would give you this whole meadow if you'd let me."

But he knew not to rush her. It would take time to win back Elizabeth's confidence and love, but he was determined to try. He'd become a new William, just for her. Eventually Elizabeth would see that he was no longer selfish and impatient, no longer proud and controlling.

For now, he would respect her wishes and stay away from her. But that didn't mean he was going to give up. He still had every intention of letting her know that he loved her. He could still send her a token of his love—the new love he'd learned to express. Never again would he frighten Elizabeth with his mother's roses. A new man inside, he'd change his outside habits too.

Quickly and quietly William began to wade

through the meadow, gathering wildflowers by the armful. He recognized the daisies and the black-eyed Susans, but there were so many others that he didn't know the names of. Some were as red as Elizabeth's lips and some as blue as her eyes. Some were as pink as her cheeks when she was flustered, and others were as golden as her hair in the sunlight. The brilliant natural colors were perfect for Elizabeth . . . they *were* Elizabeth.

He hugged the flowers to his chest and closed his eyes. Now if only he could think of words adequate to accompany the flowers. He needed a poem or a note. Not Shakespeare—he'd used the sonnets before with Elizabeth. This time he would use his own words. But what words? Were there words powerful enough to express how he felt? He lay back in the cool meadow and stared up at the stars. Slowly stroking a pink bud against his face, he imagined Elizabeth's cheek against his own. Touching a red bloom to his lips, he closed his eyes and began composing the perfect note in his mind.

Chapter
Five

"Wake up, sleepyhead," Elizabeth sang out Wednesday morning as she let herself into the dorm room after returning from the cafeteria. "I've already had my breakfast, and here you are still asleep."

She yanked back Jessica's purple comforter to reveal a teddy bear, a fashion magazine, a wadded-up satin nightshirt, and a pair of wrinkled jeans, but no Jessica.

Elizabeth double-checked her watch. *That's odd,* she thought. She couldn't believe Jessica was out and about at nine in the morning.

She flipped the comforter back over the mess on Jessica's bed and started loading her leather backpack with extra pencils, pens, paper, and a tiny penlight that she'd need in the library archives. If she hurried, she could get in an hour of cataloging before her art-history class. She was about to hoist the pack over her shoulder when someone knocked at the door.

"That you, Jess?" Elizabeth grinned, imagining her sister standing outside the door in her robe and towel turban, surprised to find the door locked. No matter how many times Elizabeth reminded her, Jessica never took a key with her when she went to the shower room. "It's a good thing you got back before I left for the library. You'd have gotten pretty cold by five o'clock this—"

Elizabeth's sentence broke when she jerked open the door. Instead of a shower-fresh Jessica, she was met by a walking floral arrangement. She could only assume there was a delivery person behind it. Because all she could see were two hands, two legs, and a virtual wall of white snapdragons and champagne sweetheart roses, accented with the mandatory baby's breath and a forest of assorted greenery.

Oh my gosh, what has William done now? she wondered.

"Flowers for Elizabeth Wakefield," came a voice from somewhere within the bouquet.

"I'm Elizabeth Wakefield," she answered. She propped the door open with her hip and took the large, blown-glass urn from the outstretched hands. "Thanks," she called out to the anonymous delivery person. Unable to see a thing over the top of the snapdragons, she waddled over to her desk

84

and set the bouquet down. She was stunned that William would have sent her such a huge arrangement. It was a far cry from his usual elegant—though unsettling—white roses.

She plucked the card from its plastic pitchfork holder, wondering if it would include a Shakespearean sonnet. His flowers always had before. "With all my love . . . Tom?" she read aloud.

She stepped back and examined the bouquet again. Tom had never sent her *anything* like this before. But of course the flowers would be from her own boyfriend. Why had she jumped to the conclusion that the flowers were from William? It was just a slip of the mind. Just a reaction to seeing the roses—although they weren't technically white, they were so pale, they'd probably registered as white in her subconscious.

It wasn't as if she'd *expected* William to send her flowers. And surely she didn't *want* him to. Did she?

"No!" she answered herself aloud. "I don't want William to send me flowers. I don't want *anything* from William White. These are from *Tom*," she repeated, as if hearing the actual words would shove thoughts of William from her mind. "How sweet of him to try and make up for our last fight this way."

She buried her face in the bouquet but jerked back when the vinegary, hothouse-flower smell stung her nose. Her shoulders sank with disappointment. She was trying to be grateful and happy, but really! This floral monstrosity was so big, it looked as if it should be propped up against a casket somewhere. Why would Tom think she'd want a bunch of gaudy, expensive, hothouse flowers? Didn't he know her better than that?

Behind her someone cleared his throat noisily. "How do you like them?"

Elizabeth whirled around in shock.

Tom pushed the door the rest of the way open and strutted into the room. "Aren't they something? I told the florist that I wanted the biggest, most impressive bunch of flowers he could come up with—something that would really knock your socks off. When he showed me a picture of Sweetheart Arrangement Number Fifteen, I knew you'd go wild about it—especially those roses. I couldn't wait to get over here and see the look on your face."

He was positively beaming with pride. And the more he gushed about the flowers, the guiltier Elizabeth felt.

When she finally dared to meet his eyes, Tom's face fell. "Well? What's wrong? Don't you like the flowers?"

"Yes, of course I do. They're beautiful."

Apparently she hadn't sounded enthusiastic enough to suit him. His lower lip pooched out and his shoulders sagged. He looked like a little kid who'd been told there was no more Disney-land.

"You *don't* like them," he accused.

"Yes, I *do* like them. I said I did, didn't I?"

"But you didn't say it like you *meant* it."

She swallowed back her annoyance and tried to sound more sincere. "Tom, the flowers were a beautiful surprise. They're really elegant and . . . uh . . . *big.* I'm *overwhelmed* that you'd go to so much trouble for me. Thank you so much."

"Great," he said with a sneer. "Now you're making fun of me." He crossed his arms and continued to pout.

Elizabeth gritted her teeth. *I can't deal with his juvenile temper tantrums now,* she thought. *I don't have the time or the patience.* She stepped around him and picked up her backpack.

Tom caught her by the elbow and spun her around. "Just what is it you want from me, Liz? Nothing I say or do anymore is good enough for you."

She pulled her arm free and sighed tiredly. "Tom, I hate to rush, but I'm late. I've got to get to—"

"Let me guess, to the *library.*"

"As a matter of fact, yes. I was actually on my way out the door when the delivery guy came."

"Fine!" he barked. "Don't let me detain you from your important research."

The hurt in his soft brown eyes nagged at her,

but no worse than her own conscience. She *had* been avoiding Tom lately, but she couldn't help it. Not only was she upset about her William White CyberDreams—not to mention his sudden reintroduction into her life—but it seemed as if her relationship with Tom had turned to utter boredom. All they ever did was sit around and study or watch TV—or fight. The fighting, that was the worst. But was it all really Tom's fault? Probably not. She silently promised herself to try harder—when she had more time.

She worked up a semblance of a smile. "I'll call you later, when I get back, OK?"

The door's reverberating slam was her only answer. Tom was already gone.

Looking at the flowers as if they were to blame, Elizabeth sighed with frustration. *What is happening to us?* she wondered. *Why can't we even speak to each other without getting angry anymore?*

"This is it!" Jessica cried. "This is the exact dress I've been looking for."

"Finally," Lila Fowler groaned.

Jessica ignored her best friend and admired herself from every angle in the dressing room's floor-length triple mirror. The strapless, embroidered satin sheath couldn't have fit any better if it had been custom-made for her. It showed off her every curve to its best advantage.

"And this matching shawl . . ." Jessica draped it

dramatically over one shoulder. "Don't you just love it?"

Lila tossed back her brunette curls with a bored expression. "I liked the black one better."

"Which black one?"

"The black crepe with the diagonal shoulder strap that you tried on in Lisette's—about fifty dresses ago."

Jessica shook her head. "I don't want black. Everyone wears black. I want to show up in the crowd. I want to *dazzle* these showbiz people like they've never been dazzled before."

"Then that little number should do it. I imagine you'll be the only one there looking like a big, grape Popsicle."

Jessica glared at Lila. "It's not *grape*, it's royal purple—my favorite color, as you well know."

Lila leaned her shoulder against the wall and crossed her arms. In her bubble-gum pink, retro capri pants and matching sweater set, she looked as if she'd just stepped off the set of a *Grease* revival. It was a very un-Lila look. But Jessica hadn't criticized her, had she? Not out loud, at least.

Choosing to ignore her friend, Jessica stepped out of the dress and double-checked the price tag. She tried not to let her wince show.

But Lila was too perceptive. She rolled her eyes dramatically. "Let me guess—you can't afford it. So now we'll have to traipse through ten more stores?"

"Of course I can afford it!" Jessica insisted indignantly. *If I don't pay my tuition next semester,* she added to herself. But she couldn't worry about that now. Next semester was a long way off, while the IM Awards were only two days away. *A person has to have priorities,* she thought as she slipped her yellow sundress back over her head.

Lila was still snarly moments later when Jessica laid the dress across the counter. "She'll take it," she told the salesclerk haughtily. "Though I shudder to think what accessories my color-blind friend will come up with."

Evidently the clerk didn't pick up on Lila's sarcasm. "We have dyed-to-match shoes," she said, zipping the purple formal into a garment bag. She handed Jessica a small white card. "If you'll just fill out your size and the heel height you want, we can have them ready for you by Friday morning."

"Perfect!" Jessica chimed. She filled out the card and handed it over with her check while Lila stood by impatiently, tapping her foot. Jessica didn't care. She was way too happy to worry about Lila's surliness.

"Where are you going?" Lila asked as they emerged from Mais Oui. "The parking garage is this way."

"I know, but the Diamond Galleria is *this* way."

"Nuh-uh." Lila dug in her heels and stopped stubbornly. "You have your dress and your shoes. Now let's go home."

90

"Lila, I'm not putting together an outfit for an insignificant high-school prom. If I'm going to schmooze with celebs, I have to look perfect from head to toe. I need *jewelry*."

"No more shopping!" Lila whined. "My feet are killing me."

"That's what you get for trying to do serious shopping in tacky platform mules!"

"Don't you dare call my shoes tacky, Jessica Wakefield. These are Pitacci originals from Italy! Besides, my shoes aren't the problem. *You* are. You've been dragging me all over this mall since ten in the morning! I'm tired of tromping around all these chintzy little stores, and I'm tired of hearing about Charles Sampson and the IM Awards."

Jessica looked at her best friend in amazement. "What's your problem today, Li? You usually love shopping as much as I do—more, since you've got the funds to actually buy things. I mean, really! Who else but you would have used her once-in-a-lifetime chance to live a virtual-reality adventure and instead choose to dream about shopping?"

"I guess CyberDreams quenched my shopping desires for a while," Lila said testily.

"Right. I believe that. And what are you going to wear to the next Theta party? A virtual dress?"

Lila rolled her eyes and Jessica rolled hers back. She had no idea what was going on in her friend's snooty, overallowanced brain, but she was definitely getting tired of it. Imagine Lila acting as if shopping were a bad thing!

"Lila, I've got to have jewelry. It's like . . . a requirement!"

"One more store, Jessica. That's my limit!"

Jessica happily dragged her friend off to the Diamond Galleria, where a roly-poly man in a Mr. Rogers sweater met them at the door and ushered them inside as if he were welcoming them into his home.

"Miss Fowler!" he gushed as their eyes adjusted to the dim interior lights. "How wonderful to see you again."

Jessica wasn't surprised that the jeweler would know Lila's name. Lila's shopping sprees probably kept half the stores in Sweet Valley Mall afloat.

"What can I do for you today?" As he bowed and scraped, Jessica noticed that he had one strand of hair swirled around and around the top of his pink, bald head.

"Nothing for me today, Mr. Evert," Lila said grandly. "My friend here is just *looking*."

Mr. Evert's face sagged—just a little, but enough that Jessica could tell he didn't think she'd be the kind of valued customer Lila was.

"Well, you two ladies go ahead and look around. Let me know if I can be of any assistance." He scurried back to the rear of the store, stuck one of those funny lens thingies on his eye, and busied himself with some jewelry repair.

Lila stopped in front of the very first display case she came to and tapped on the glass with a perfectly manicured fingernail. "What about this one?"

Jessica leaned in for a closer look. "Emeralds? Oh, right. Green and purple. That'd be just *gorgeous,* Lila," she said sarcastically. "I'd prefer something that will turn heads, not stomachs."

Lila covered a bored yawn, then shrugged. "I'm just trying to help."

"No, you're not. You're just picking any old thing, hoping I'll hurry up and let you go home. But you know what? I'm finally beginning to see through your little game. It's not the shopping that's bothering you. You just don't want me to look good at the IM Awards because you're *jealous.* You can't stand the thought of me spending time with movie stars and famous directors when you're going to be sitting around in Boredomville with Mr. Supersnob, Bruce Patman."

"I'm not jealous of your silly date, Jessica. I'm just tired!"

"Well, if you'll help me find a decent necklace, we can get out of here. And please try to find one in the same color neighborhood as my dress."

"OK, I'll yell if I see a gold chain with plastic grapes dangling from it."

Jessica gave Lila the dirtiest look she could manage. "What about something like this?" Jessica pointed to a large, Victorian-style choker of rhine-stones and amethysts.

"That tacky thing!" Lila cried. "If you're going to go all out, you might as well at least make a statement." She pointed to a diamond teardrop pendant. "Here's what you need."

"Right, like I could afford that in *this* lifetime."

"What do you want, Jess? Something you can afford or something that will wow them?" Lila pulled a tube of lipstick from her impossibly tiny purse and began to apply a coat of magenta to her lips. "Just charge it," she mumbled through lips otherwise occupied. "That's what I always do." She finished with a loud smack.

"Lila, the dress practically cleared out my whole checking account. I can't afford anything like this."

"Then why are we bothering to look? Let's go home."

"I don't suppose you have a necklace I could borrow?"

"I don't own a thing that would look good with a *purple* dress. Besides, you've seen every-thing I have with me at school. Most of my good pieces are stored in the vault at Fowler Crest. Daddy would absolutely throw a fit if I took any of it out to lend you."

"Your father likes me."

"Jessica, you're my very best friend in the whole world. But my father has absolutely forbidden me

94

to loan you any of my *real* jewelry. It's an insurance thing—you wouldn't understand."

Jessica pursed her lips and tried to decide if she wanted to strangle Lila or just smack her. She settled for a verbal slap. "Forget it. All of your jewelry is too gaudy anyway. I just asked because you're the only friend I have who has tons of the stuff."

Lila didn't seem to take offense. "If you're dead set on borrowing jewelry, why don't you just borrow a necklace from a *store*? The stars do it for award shows all the time. It's no big deal for them. Some jewelers shell out millions in jewelry every year just for the advertising."

"That's a great idea. Why don't you talk to your friend over there and see if he'll lend me this pendant?"

Lila's whine grated on Jessica's ears like nails on a chalkboard. "Jessica, I'm exhausted. If you want a necklace, *you* go talk to Mr. Evert yourself!" Lila shouldered her expensive leather bag and started for the door.

"Li! You can't desert me in my time of need."

Lila waggled her fingers over her shoulder without looking back. "Ta ta. Don't worry about driving me back to campus. I'll take a taxi. You stay as long as you want."

"Go ahead, traitor," Jessica mumbled as her ex–best friend walked prissily out the door. "I don't need your help. I'll do it myself; you'll see.

The IM Awards are way too important to let a spoiled, rich, jealous prima donna spoil the day."

Jessica raised her head haughtily. Mimicking Lila's saunter without even realizing it, she walked to the rear of the store, where Mr. Evert hovered over a broken bracelet.

She cleared her throat discreetly, then plunged ahead. "Excuse me, Mr. Evert," she said, letting her long, blond hair fall seductively across her face and sweep along the glass display case.

He looked up with surprise.

"I don't believe we've met. I'm Lila Fowler's best friend, Jessica Wakefield."

The jeweler looked nonplussed. "And?"

"And have I got a deal for you!"

"Yes, I'm *positive*," Elizabeth said for the third time. She'd been on the phone with John Petrie for the past fifteen minutes, and their conversation was starting to wear thin. He seemed obsessed with the idea that there was a rat living in the archives. Even worse, he seemed to think she was personally responsible for bringing it there.

"Yes, I was working in the records room earlier today, but I promise you, I didn't smuggle any food down there with me." She drummed impatiently on her desktop with her pencil eraser. "No, not even a candy bar."

While he reiterated the danger of having a rodent loose in the presence of important historical books and papers, Elizabeth propped the receiver against her shoulder and held it with her ear so she could use both hands to stack the papers that littered the top of her usually clean desk. She'd been trying to make some order out of the jumble of notes she'd taken in the archives earlier today.

"Uh-huh, I can see where that would be a big problem," she agreed when John paused for a breath. "But all the files I've cataloged so far have been in relatively good condition. Some have been rather crumbly and yellow, and a couple have been mildew stained. But I haven't seen anything that even vaguely looked like it'd been chewed by rats."

She sighed when he once more launched into a detailed description of the signs to look for. *How am I ever going to get all this work done?* she thought with annoyance.

"No, I haven't found anything like that. . . . Strange noises? . . . No, I haven't heard any bumping or scratching in the walls. . . . No. No strange smells either . . .

"Actually, I've been so wrapped up in the excitement of my work, I probably wouldn't have seen a rat if it'd skittered across my feet."

That was an extreme exaggeration, but Elizabeth was more than ready to change the subject. It worked. John asked her how the work was going.

"I'm making lots of progress," she assured him. "I plan to go back later today, but I wanted to get some of these notes in order before I went." She paused, hoping he'd take the hint and let her get back to work.

He didn't. Instead John began telling her about all the paperwork the new archives project was creating for his staff.

Desperate to end their conversation, Elizabeth was about to make up an excuse of some sort when fate came to the rescue.

"Oh, John, I'm going to have to hang up now," she said, grateful for the interruption. "Someone is at my door." Elizabeth stood up, sending an avalanche of papers sliding from her desk to the floor. She grabbed for them and nearly dropped the phone. But John's voice rattled on in her ear.

"Really, John, I have to go answer the door," she interrupted. "I'll talk to you later, OK? Bye-bye." She said it all in one breath so he wouldn't have an opportunity to break in and start talking again. She hung up with a sigh of relief and hurried to the door.

But she was too late. She poked her head into the hallway, hoping she could catch whoever it'd been as they walked away. The hall was empty—except on the floor near her feet lay a bouquet of wildflowers.

"My favorites!" Elizabeth cried, picking up the flowers and cradling them in her arms. As their sweet perfume engulfed her, she smiled. Just when she'd begun to think her relationship with Tom was hopeless, he had proved that he still knew how to please her. The fact that he'd actually gone out and handpicked flowers for her meant more than words of apology.

"Oh, Tom," she whispered, wishing he were there in person so she could really show him how pleased she was. These flowers were so much more beautiful than that hideous arrangement.

Stepping back into her room, she looked around for something to put the bouquet in. Her gaze landed on the blown-glass vase holding the gaudy sweetheart arrangement. *No,* she told herself. *That would be too mean.* Maybe she had a jar or basket or something in the top of her closet.

As she set the flowers on the corner of her bed to look, a note fell to the floor. She picked it up and read:

> Though I dwell in darkness,
> you bring light to my heart
> and sunshine to my soul.

How beautiful, she thought. The darkness part didn't make much sense, but Tom could be very poetic and sentimental when he tried. He'd written some eloquent and passionate poems for her when they first met. He hadn't done anything that romantic in ages.

She continued to read.

I present nature's true beauties
to nature's truest beauty.
I promise,
no more white roses.

Her eyes opened wide. She looked from the note to the flowers and then back to the note. The wildflowers were from William!

Her hands began to tremble at the very thought of finishing the note. What horrifying threat would follow? It was William's pattern; she'd seen it all before. Flowers, notes, threats, then what?

Slowly she forced her eyes down the rest of the page:

If you think you ever can forgive me . . .
if there's even a glimmer of hope,
please meet me in the library at 2:00.
I'll be waiting in the basement.
But if you can't come,

Elizabeth held her breath.

I'll understand.

Relief flooded over Elizabeth, and her pounding heart slowed back to normal. There were no demands, no threats in the note—just a simple invitation.

Maybe he has *changed*, Elizabeth thought, picking up the wildflowers once more. She breathed deeply, taking in their perfume. Despite their origin, she loved the flowers. Their natural, honest colors were so bright and beautiful compared to Tom's washed-out hybrids. More than that, they made her feel happy—something she hadn't felt in ages.

Should she take a chance and go meet William? Did he deserve a second chance? Could he be trusted? All these questions swirled through Elizabeth's mind. She was tempted to answer yes to all of them. After all, the library was a public place. And she had to go over there later anyway. And at least William seemed to know what kind of flowers she liked—unlike *some* people.

Suddenly the door burst open. Jessica skidded into the room. "Liz!" she shouted. "I'm so glad I caught you!"

Uh-oh, Elizabeth thought, noting the large, fancy garment bag from Mais Oui draped over Jessica's arm. *My sister has gone crazy at the mall again and needs a loan.*

"I don't have any extra cash lying around, if that's what you're after, Jess."

"I don't need your money."

Elizabeth feigned shock.

"Don't kid around. This is serious—life and death," Jessica exclaimed. "You are the only one who can help me!"

Chapter Six

"Please, please, please!" Jessica pleaded. She knew only too well that skeptical, uncooperative look on her sister's face. Sometimes Elizabeth could be the stubbornest person on the planet. "What do you want me to do, get down on my knees and beg?" Jessica pressed her hands together like a praying child.

"Jessica, the whole thing sounds silly. Besides, I just don't have time to go to the mall. I have to get all this information from the archives sorted. Plus I haven't even started reading the material for my English-lit paper."

"C'mon, Liz. You don't understand. How else could someone like me get an expensive necklace for one night? And this isn't *silly*. It's a totally foolproof plan. I guarantee nothing can go wrong. But you've got to come to the jewelry store with me and talk to the guy. I can't do this myself. I just don't know the right things to say."

Jessica pulled the mangy-looking flowers from her sister's arms and laid them on the edge of her desk. She was tired of Elizabeth fiddling with them and not paying attention to her. "Believe me, I tried," she continued. "When I asked that snooty Mr. Evert at the Diamond Galleria, he just turned up his little pug nose at me. I couldn't believe it. Not after the way he'd been fawning all over Lila from the moment we walked in the door. If she'd asked him, he'd probably have loaned her the whole crummy store, but not me." Jessica looked at herself in the mirror and lifted her hands in puzzlement. "I don't get it. Store owners just take one look at me and think I'm a flighty blonde who can't be trusted."

"No, *really?*"

Jessica's mouth dropped open. "Hey, not fair!"

"Just kidding, Jess," Elizabeth said soothingly. "But seriously, if that's the case, then why do you think they'd listen to me? You and I look exactly alike."

"Not *exactly*," Jessica insisted.

"Jess, in case you've forgotten, we're *identical* twins."

"True, but you come off different." Jessica placed her hands on her hips. "Don't give me that 'she's crazy' look. You know you do. Personally, *I* don't see it, but you must have an aura or something."

Elizabeth shook her head. "You're the only person I know who could come up with something as lame as an *aura* to get her own way."

"You know what I mean. You've got that responsibility thing going on. It's always been different for you. Adults trust you on sight."

"But—"

Jessica grabbed her sister's arm and tugged on it. "Come on. You could convince any jeweler in the mall. I know you could."

"Jessica, why don't you borrow something from Lila?" Elizabeth pulled her arm free. "She's got enough jewelry to open her own store—and she's even got all those countess things."

"I already told you; Lila was being a witch all morning. She wouldn't loan me a dress. She wouldn't loan me any jewelry, and she wouldn't even talk to that Diamond Galleria guy for me. All she did was whine and complain. I didn't understand a thing she was babbling about— something about shopping making her feel like her virtual-reality dream was coming true."

Elizabeth suddenly looked as if she were about to faint.

"What's wrong? Don't tell me you had shopping nightmares too."

"No, but I can see how Lila could be upset about those stupid CyberDreams . . . even if they were about shopping."

"Well, I can't. It was all just a bunch of computer

mumbo jumbo. I don't know why everybody's letting it get to them. That creep Jonah Falk had a lot of nerve even coming here." She smiled suddenly. "I hope he sees me on TV Friday night. Then he can eat his heart out knowing what he passed up. Especially when he sees me all decked out in magnificent jewels. *Please*, Elizabeth. Come to the mall with me!"

Elizabeth shook her head stubbornly.

"You can't do this. You can't abandon me the way Lila did! You're my sister. My older sister."

"By four whole minutes."

"I need your help. C'mon, Liz. Be a pal. I'll never ask you for another thing as long as I live!"

Elizabeth rolled her eyes. "Wow, like I've never heard *that* line before."

Jessica sighed. It was time to pull out the big guns. "I'll clean my side of the room and I'll empty the wastebaskets every morning for a month."

"You *should* empty them every day since I fill them picking up *your* junk."

Jessica nodded enthusiastically. "I will. I'll empty them . . . *twice* a day. I'll even clean the sink every morning after I brush my teeth."

"Excuse me? Hello? Jess, we share the bathroom with the rest of the floor!" Elizabeth laughed and picked up her crappy flowers again. "I have to put these in water. They're starting to wilt."

"Don't try to change the subject. I'm serious. I'll do anything if you'll just help me." Jessica racked her brain to remember their last argument. Oh, right—it had been over one of Elizabeth's pet peeves. "If you'll come to the mall and help me, I'll even put gas in the Jeep every single time I drive it."

"That would be a pleasant change," Elizabeth admitted.

Bull's-eye, Jessica thought, seeing a glimmer in her sister's eye and hearing the faint change of tone in her voice. She could practically see Elizabeth bending to her will. "Then you'll do it?" she coaxed. "If I remember to put gas in the Jeep from now on, you'll go to the mall with me and help me get a necklace?"

Elizabeth picked at the flowers. "Well . . . I don't know, Jess. Maybe . . . let me think about it."

Yessss! "Thanks, Liz. You are the only one around here who seems to know how important this is to me—"

"Whoa, wait just a minute," Elizabeth interrupted. "I haven't said I'd do it—just that I'd think about it."

But Jessica knew she had her hooked. She could feel it—it was time to clinch the deal. "Listen, I know I've been—" Suddenly a knock at the door diverted Elizabeth's attention. *What rotten timing!* Jessica fumed. "Listen, Elizabeth, I—"

"Just a second, Jess. Let's see who's at the door."

Jessica threw up her hands in exasperation. She almost had Elizabeth convinced. She was one lousy promise away from getting what she wanted, and some—some—*door knocker* had to go and ruin everything. "Don't answer it. Whoever it is will go away."

"Whoever it is might be bringing us our ten-million-dollar check from Publishers Clearing House."

"Hard-ly! Please, at least give me your answer first. Promise you'll come to the mall with me."

"Jessica, open the door already!"

Jessica jumped in the way, trying to block her sister's path to the door. "Promise first."

But Elizabeth simply ignored her and reached for the doorknob.

Tom stood in the hallway outside room 28 and shifted impatiently from his left foot to his right. Maybe he was acting like a fool, but he just couldn't give up so easily on his relationship with Elizabeth. It was way too precious to him.

He'd made it almost all the way back to his room before he'd decided to go back and try to work things out. Not even daring to waste the time it'd take to walk back across campus, he'd jumped into his car and sped straight to Dickenson Hall. Now after all that rushing, it seemed to be taking forever for someone to answer the door.

"Come on," he muttered. "I know you're in

there." He could hear voices behind the door—Jessica's, if he wasn't mistaken. What was taking so long?

He knocked once more, rapping his knuckles so hard against the door, they hurt. "Come on, Elizabeth. I know you're furious with me, but the least you can do is hear me out."

Just as he reached up to knock a third time, the door was jerked open by Elizabeth, who stood there holding his flowers.

Tom smiled. But his attention was quickly drawn from Elizabeth to Jessica as she shoved past him and through the doorway.

"Excuse me! I'm going to the bathroom," she announced rudely. "I hope you two can wrap this up fast. *Some* people already have plans for this afternoon!"

As if I care! he thought as he watched Jessica tear down the hallway. When it seemed safe, he looked back at Elizabeth. She didn't seem very happy to see him. And now that he was looking at her more carefully, he realized that the flowers in her arms weren't the ones he'd bought at all. They were just cheap, tacky flowers that someone had picked from a yard somewhere—barely a step up from weeds.

"Where'd you get those ugly things?" he asked.

Elizabeth bristled. "Someone left them outside my door."

"Who?" he demanded sharply.

"I don't think it's any of your business, Tom Watts."

"Well, I think it is." Jealousy crowded out his common sense. His hands clenched into fists. "I knew it! You're seeing someone else behind my back, aren't you?"

Lifting her dainty chin belligerently, Elizabeth glared at him. "What if I am?" she said at last.

Tom dug his nails into the palms of his hands and fought for control. He'd nearly lost Elizabeth before because of his temper. He couldn't let it happen again. He swallowed hard and tried to relax his tensing muscles.

"I'm sorry, Liz," he said finally. "I'm just in a bad mood, I guess."

But Elizabeth just stood there with one hand full of flowers and the other on the door, as if she were ready to slam it in his face.

"I said I'm sorry," he repeated. "I—"

"I *heard* what you said," Elizabeth snapped, cutting off his apology. "But you know something? I don't really care right now."

"What?"

"You can't waltz in here, yell accusations at me, then suddenly turn on your charm and expect me to instantly forgive and forget. I'm *angry*, Tom. And I want you to leave."

"Whoa! Back up the temper train! Don't you think it would be better for both of us if we talked this out?" He reached out for her, but just as his fingers grazed the soft skin of her arm, she edged away.

"What would be better for *me* is for you to go away and let me sort things out for myself."

"What's to sort out? I acted like a jerk. I apologized. Problem solved."

"Tom, stop bothering me. Please."

"Jeez! What's gotten into you lately?" he asked. "Give a guy a chance, would you? This isn't like you, Liz. Not at all."

"What do *you* know about what's like me! Sometimes I think you don't know me at all!"

As she nudged him in the chest, Tom had no choice but to step backward into the hallway. The last thing he noticed before the door slammed loudly in his face was that she still clutched those stinking wildflowers in her arms as if they were some great treasure.

Furious, Elizabeth yanked Tom's flowers out of their urn, dropped them into the wastebasket, and put the wildflowers in their place.

"He doesn't own me!" she ranted. "How *dare* he come in here and accuse me of seeing someone else? I've never been unfaithful to Tom. . . ." But a pang of guilt broke into her little tirade. Maybe she wasn't being entirely truthful. Wasn't having the CyberDream fantasy about William a little like being unfaithful? Hadn't she just moments ago been considering the possibility of meeting William at the library?

Have I been unfaithful in my mind? she wondered guiltily. Suddenly contrite, she bent down and picked up Tom's flowers, but the very sight and smell of them annoyed her all over again.

It was more than just the flowers. From anyone else they might have been an appreciated token. But Tom was supposed to know her. Why couldn't he make an effort? *She* had. She was always thinking about his feelings . . . his likes and dislikes. She never asked him to take her out for Chinese food. Why? Because he preferred Mexican or pizza. How many times had she bypassed a romantic movie because he liked spies and car chases? She knew how he preferred his coffee . . . what television programs he watched . . . his favorite music. She knew everything about him.

"And how well does he know me? He thinks I like funeral flowers!" She gave the flowers a choking squeeze as if they were to blame.

And why was Tom being so pushy all of a sudden? And needy? And clingy? One of the things she'd always loved about her relationship with Tom was that they gave each other enough space to live their own lives. But lately he'd been so possessive and jealous, she felt constantly smothered.

She looked at the flowers again and wrinkled her nose. "Well, I can't stand here holding these trashy things all day," she muttered. She picked up a large, but somewhat dented, popcorn bucket from under Jessica's desk and plunked Tom's flowers into it. "There!" She propped the slightly disheveled bouquet on top of the radiator—more on Jessica's side than hers. "That's more than you deserve. These ugly things prove you don't care about me, Tom Watts. And if you don't care . . . then neither do I."

Elizabeth picked a black-eyed Susan from William's bouquet and tucked it through the strap of her backpack. It was just the thing to brighten the dreary archives room.

Maybe I should *go meet William . . . just to see what he has to say. If he* has *changed, then I could be passing up—*

"Are you ready to help me now?" Jessica bellowed from the doorway.

Elizabeth sighed. "This is not a good time for me."

"What's the deal? You *promised!*"

Elizabeth opened her eyes wide with surprise. "Refresh my memory here, Jess. Exactly *when* did I promise to go to the mall and help you con some poor jeweler out of his livelihood?"

"Right before Prince Tom marched in here like he owned the place." Jessica plopped down in her desk chair and scooted Tom's flowers toward Elizabeth's side of the radiator. "He told you not to help me, didn't he? Really, Elizabeth! Get some backbone. You shouldn't let him control your life."

113

"Jessica, I didn't *promise* you. And Tom isn't controlling my life. He doesn't even know about your little scheme."

"Oh, I see. Then it's all your idea to renege on your promise. Where's your loyalty?" Jessica put on her poutiest expression. "This is really below you. I can't believe you'd refuse to go to the mall with me just because you'd rather go somewhere with Tom."

"I'm not going anywhere with Tom! Jess, you're getting all worked up over nothing." Elizabeth closed her eyes and gave up. As much as she really didn't want to go to the mall, she didn't want to spend the rest of the day arguing with her sister even more. Besides, Elizabeth was fighting a losing battle. She knew from experience that Jessica wasn't likely to give up. She'd whine, plead, and nag until the inevitable happened. Jessica would always get her own way in the end.

Elizabeth opened her eyes to see Jessica smiling over her with her purse in her hand.

Oh, well, what could it hurt? It wouldn't cost anything more than gas money, and if she failed, she could always tell Jessica that she tried. And if by some miracle she was able to convince some unsuspecting jeweler to lend Jessica a necklace, then her twin would be on cloud nine. Either way, she'd quit bugging Elizabeth about it.

"OK, I'll help you—"

Jessica's smile spread from ear to ear. "Let's go!"

"Wait a second. I can't go to a ritzy jewelry store looking like this. My jeans are dusty from working in the archives, and I—"

"You look fine."

"That's a switch. Usually you're griping at me to update my wardrobe or fix my hair."

"OK, OK. Change clothes. But hurry, will you? I can't wait to get back to the mall."

Elizabeth hardly had time to open her closet door before Jessica's patience ran out.

"Here, wear this," Jessica said. She grabbed her sky blue denim skirt off the bedpost, where it had landed during her closet clean out. "It'll go great with that top you have on, so you won't even have to change shirts."

Elizabeth dutifully slipped out of her jeans and stepped into the skirt.

"Your hair is fine," Jessica said quickly before Elizabeth had time to check it in the mirror.

"Oh? Really? So now you *like* my ponytail?"

"Yes. I love it. Now, come on. Let's go!"

Elizabeth smiled. She really loved her twin, even if she made her crazy at times. And it was nearly impossible to be depressed when Jessica was around. "I'm coming. I'm coming. Let me grab my purse."

As Elizabeth reached across her desk, she looked once again at the wildflowers. *I'm sorry, William, but you'll just have to wait,* she thought. *Sisters come first. I hope you don't get too mad.*

The thought chilled her for a moment. Elizabeth had learned the hard way that it wasn't a good idea to make William White mad. But if he really had changed, then it wouldn't be that big a deal, right?

Tom paused at the door of his blue Saturn and looked back toward Dickenson Hall. He could just imagine Elizabeth all alone in her room—sad and upset. His first instinct was to go back upstairs and try to reason with her. But he knew it would only make matters worse. She'd been so touchy lately.

Still, he knew he was partly to blame. He hadn't meant to lose his temper. But she could be so exasperating sometimes! Maybe he should go back.

He swallowed loudly and squared his shoulders. It was definitely worth a try. But he'd hardly taken a step before he froze with surprise. The dorm's back door opened, and Jessica rushed out. Elizabeth was close on her heels.

Tom hunkered down so he couldn't be seen. "I thought she wanted to sit in her room and sort things out," he grumbled under his breath. "Sure, she did. What a crock!"

Tom watched as Jessica and Elizabeth hurried across the parking lot to their red Jeep. They seemed happy enough. Jessica was telling some story that required a lot of hand gestures, and

Elizabeth was laughing her pretty head off. Neither sister seemed to be the least bit upset.

Where could they be going in such a hurry?

Tom slid behind the wheel of his car as anger washed over him like a wave of nausea. He didn't want to feel this way, but his brain had kicked into jealousy gear and there was no turning back.

Something else about Elizabeth's appearance bothered him, but it took him a few moments to realize what it was. He slammed his hands against the steering wheel. She had changed clothes, that's what. "Where on earth did she get that ridiculously short skirt?" he said. He'd never seen her wear anything like that before. Five minutes ago she'd had on jeans. He was sure of it! She probably got dressed up to meet someone! Even the fact that Elizabeth was with her sister didn't ease his mind, especially as Jessica's words echoed in his brain:

"Some *people already have plans for this afternoon!*"

"I'll just *bet* she has plans," Tom mumbled. "Elizabeth is probably going to drop Jessica somewhere and then go off and meet her new boyfriend—the cheap jerk who gives her bouquets of weeds."

Distrust churned his stomach to a boil. Sweat popped out across his forehead. He started the car and flicked the air conditioner to high, but even with the sudden blast of air in his face, he was steaming. "When I find out who this guy is, I'm gonna . . ."

But how would he ever find out? Elizabeth wouldn't tell him. She was hardly even speaking to him anymore.

As the Wakefields' Jeep backed from its spot, Tom made his decision. With his jaw set in a tight, firm line and his hands clenched on the steering wheel, he pulled away from the curb and followed them.

Chapter Seven

Where is she? William wondered. *What could have happened?*

He poked his arm out of the shadows and into a pool of quivering fluorescent light long enough to read his watch. Two-twenty. It was so unlike Elizabeth to be late. She was punctual to a fault. He choked back his fury and slunk deeper into the shadows.

Hearing a rumble and thunk as the library's air conditioner kicked on, he shivered. It was chilly down in the basement. He needed to move around and get his blood flowing. With a sigh he resumed his pacing. He'd already been waiting in the stacks for thirty minutes.

Dr. Denby had warned him that she might not come, but that didn't make it any easier to accept. William clenched and unclenched his fists. He could feel the tension starting in his neck and working its way down through his arms to his fingers.

Suddenly he could almost hear Dr. Denby's voice telling him to control his anger. *Modern psychiatry at its best,* William thought as he struggled to obey. He began to whisper directions to himself almost like a mantra. "I won't lose my temper. I'm in control. I will stay calm. . . ." His temper had always been one of his worst qualities in the past, one that he'd worked very hard to change. But sometimes it was nearly impossible to control it, even now.

Nearing exhaustion from controlling his anger, William laid his hands against a row of books. Their familiar feel and smell helped him concentrate his energy away from his tensing muscles.

Inches away, he noticed a book of Shakespearean sonnets, inappropriately stored among the nonfiction. He'd loaned Elizabeth that exact book once. He pulled it off the shelf and hugged it to his chest. Just touching something he knew she'd held made him feel calmer.

Maybe Elizabeth is testing me, he told himself. *Maybe she's not coming on purpose—just to see if I'll blow it. She wants to know if I've changed enough to stay calm. Well, I'll show her I have. I will not lose my temper. I will prove to her that the evil inside me no longer exists.*

He opened the book to a sonnet he knew she loved and pressed his cheek against the smooth, cool page. "I forgive you, Elizabeth," he whispered. "I forgive you for standing me up. I forgive you for feeling that you have to test me. I forgive you for being afraid, for wanting me dead . . . even for crashing me into that tree."

With an earsplitting rip the page came away in his clenched fist. Immediately William felt regret. He hadn't meant to harm the beautiful book. "I forgive you everything, Elizabeth," he whispered. "Now if only you'll forgive me."

He tucked the torn page back in place and replaced the book on the shelf. "Soon," he muttered as he returned to the shadows. "Soon you will trust me. If only you'll give me a chance, you'll see that I'm a changed man. I'm going to prove to you how much I love you . . . no matter what it takes."

Jessica grabbed her sister's elbow and steered her past the doorway of the Diamond Galleria. "We're not going in that tacky shop!" she said with as much indignation as she could muster.

"But I thought the necklace you liked was here."

"Aw, it wasn't all *that*. And anyway, why should I give that snooty Mr. Evert the benefit of my publicity? He's nothing but a loser. He'll be sorry when I'm rich and famous. After the way he snubbed me, he'll be lucky if I don't tell all my friends to take their business elsewhere."

121

"*All* your friends?" Elizabeth teased. "Lila is your only friend who could afford to shop there."

"Well, I'll tell *Lila*, then. That alone should put a big dent in his annual income." Jessica pulled her sister past the fountain and across the mall's wide, red-tiled walkway. "I've decided not to waste my time on the little guys. I'm starting at the top," she proclaimed, coming to a halt in front of R. Donantelli's Creations. She paused dramatically and waited for Elizabeth to quit gawking.

R. Donantelli's was a small but extremely expensive jewelry boutique tucked away in a quiet corner of Sweet Valley Mall, where every piece was an original, hand-created by the owner.

Elizabeth gave her one of those skeptical looks that she was so good at, but Jessica ignored it and nudged her into the serene interior of the store. The utter splendor took Jessica's breath away. Although a sparkling chandelier shone way above her head, the real glitter in the room seemed to come from hundreds of small display cases filled with sparkling diamonds, emeralds, rubies, and sapphires. The whole store was like a dark heaven, twinkling with multicolored stars.

Jessica caught the edge of Elizabeth's skirt and urged her across the marble entryway. As they tiptoed farther into the store, the thick, rich maroon carpet swallowed up the sound of their steps.

Suddenly Jessica cried out, disturbing the almost churchlike quiet of the store. "Elizabeth, look!" She jerked her sister to a halt and pointed to the most perfect necklace she'd ever seen. Below a layer of pristine, smudgeless glass lay a mesmerizing creation made up of multiple strands of antique cultured pearls, which were held together with a huge diamond clasp. She tapped frantically at the glass. "Look at that clasp! It's the same exact shape as the IM Award."

"Um, it's a *star*."

Jessica rolled her eyes. "And pray tell, Miss Entertainment Expert, what is the shape of the IM Award?"

"A star, but . . .," Elizabeth huffed. "Jess, a star is a star."

"I *know* it's a star, but it's *still* the shape of the IM Award. Don't you get it? It's an omen. It's fate. Didn't you notice how I walked straight over here to it? I have to have *this* necklace."

Elizabeth shook her head. "Did you happen to check out the price tag? I think you'd better look for an omen that's a little less expensive."

"What does that matter if we're going to *borrow* it?"

"I think you're being unrealistic."

Jessica stuck her hands on her hips. "My mind is made up. Now will you *please* go talk to that little man over there? Ask him if we can speak to the owner."

Elizabeth leaned forward until they were practically nose to nose. "I will not!"

Backing away slightly, Jessica clamped her lips in a tight line. How could her sister do this to her? She'd promised to help, and now that they'd come all this way, she was backing out. It was almost as if she'd tried to get her hopes up for nothing! "Forget it. I'll do it myself."

Jessica marched across the floor. Something of the stomping effect was lost on the soft carpet, but she knew Elizabeth would get the idea.

"Excuse me," she said to the deeply tanned, older man behind the counter. When he lifted his head to look at her, the gray in his naturally dark hair glittered almost as much as the diamonds in his lighted display cases. Jessica looked up to see if he had a special light shining above his head.

"How may I help you?" he asked. His voice was slightly accented and deep.

"I'd like to speak to someone with authority. The manager or the owner will do nicely."

"At your service, miss. I am Raoul Donantelli. Owner, manager, creator, and at the moment, salesclerk. What can I do for so pretty a lady?"

Jessica cleared her throat and tried to remember the refined voice she'd used as Lady Macbeth in a school play. "Actually, Mr. Donantelli, I'm here to do something for you."

Raoul Donantelli leaned forward with a merry but skeptical twinkle in his dark eyes while Jessica did her best to convince him to lend her the necklace.

"I'm sorry," he said after patiently listening to Jessica's whole plan. "As much as I'd like to help you, I just can't risk it."

"But there is no risk. I *promise*. I'll just wear the necklace to the award show and bring it right back. The good you'll gain from the exposure will far outweigh any risk. Think of all the publicity you'll be getting. It'll be like *free* advertising."

"I don't really see how you can help me."

Jessica wanted to scream. What had she just been explaining to this man? "How can you say that? Having your jewels showcased on the IMA telecast is like a free billboard on Times Square—no, it's better."

"No offense, my child," he said. "But who will notice a simple college girl—beautiful though you may be? Pretty girls at these Hollywood functions are as plentiful as rhinestones in that tasteless Diamond Galleria across the way. Now if you were a famous model or a beautiful movie star like Ginger Sampson, then I might agree."

Jessica leaned forward and lowered her voice. "Have you ever heard of *The Young and the Beautiful*?"

"It is a . . . soap opera?"

"It's only the most-watched daytime drama in the nation."

"Are you telling me that you're the star of this . . . drama?"

"Well . . . I used to be . . . on it." Jessica looked

125

away. She'd omitted the tiny fact that she'd only been on for a weeklong guest appearance. But she wasn't really lying.

She looked back up at him. For a moment his eyes flickered with interest, but then he wavered. He pursed his lips doubtfully.

Oh, I almost had him and then blew it! she thought. *Now what?*

"My sister was on the show too," Jessica added, hunting through her mind for any nearly true fabrication that might sway him to her way of thinking. "We played twins and got absolutely rave reviews. We'd still be on the show today except some of the bigger names were jealous of all the attention we were getting and forced us off the show. Contract negotiations and all . . . Well, you know how that goes."

Raoul Donantelli lifted a heavily ringed finger against his pursed lips and looked skeptically over the top of his little tortoiseshell reading glasses. He shook his head.

But it didn't sway her a bit. Jessica wasn't giving up. "*I'm* still interested in acting, of course, but my sister isn't. She gave it up for her career in journalism. Oh! Did I mention that my sister is a famous newspaper reporter?"

Suddenly Mr. Donantelli seemed more interested. Jessica worked on setting the hook.

"While I'm enjoying the festivities, she'll be working—covering the gala for her newspaper,"

Jessica continued. "It's so funny. Even though she's this big fancy writer, she still gets all starstruck at these things. She lets her writing get all out of proportion with too much 'who's with who' and 'who's wearing what.' Sometimes I nag at her to report the, like, hard facts and stuff. But she *insists* she writes to suit the demands of her millions of fans." Jessica brushed her hair over her shoulder and struck a thoughtful pose. "And we're so close. She's always sticking me in her stories somewhere. Sometimes it just drives me crazy."

Mr. Donantelli lifted his hand in a gesture for Elizabeth to join them and called out to her, "Is this true, young lady?"

Elizabeth, who'd been ogling a display case of engagement rings, acted as if she'd just awakened from a trance. "Huh? I mean, what?"

"You are a newspaper reporter?" Mr. Donantelli asked.

"Yes." Elizabeth grinned as if she was proud that her fame had spread all the way out to Sweet Valley Mall. She hurried over and stood beside Jessica. "I write for the Swe—*ow!*"

Jessica had stomped her toe just in time. Otherwise Elizabeth would've blabbed that she worked for the rinky-dink school paper and spoiled everything. Who would that have impressed?

Jessica hurriedly filled in the space left by

127

Elizabeth's sudden silence. "One thing you can say about Elizabeth, she's *loyal* to her sister. She loves writing about fashion trends, but if I were to wear a Donantelli original to the IM Awards, you could be sure the necklace and I would get top billing. *Right*, Elizabeth?"

Elizabeth glared at Jessica and rubbed her toe against the back of her leg. "Yeah. Right. Whenever I write about fashion, you can bet Jessica has something to do with it. Just think of her as my inspiration."

"This is going to be the biggest story of the year," Jessica added.

Donantelli scratched his head thoughtfully. "True?" he asked, his eyes now completely on Elizabeth.

Elizabeth came through like a champ. "Mr. Donantelli, you can be sure I'll fill as large a space with this story as my editor will allow."

Making an occasional "hmmm" noise, Raoul Donantelli studied Jessica, then he looked over at Elizabeth . . . then back at Jessica again. All the while he kept tapping his ring ringer against his lips as if it helped him concentrate. Jessica watched his hand, mesmerized by the diamond. It was as big as a chunk of Bubble Yum. He studied the twins a moment longer, then looked right at Jessica and sighed. "OK," he said at last. "Pick yourself a piece."

Jessica began to bounce happily.

"For the one night only," he stressed. "You must wear it to no other events."

"Oh, I won't, I promise." Jessica dashed across the store. "Here, this is the one I want!"

"That is one of my most expensive pieces," he said, as if admiring it for the first time.

Jessica held her breath as he unlocked the display case and lifted the pearl necklace as gently as if it were a baby. With a proud-papa smile he slipped it into a special monogrammed, maroon velvet jewelry case and carefully secured the clasp. "Keep the necklace in this case at all times when it is not on your pretty neck."

"Oh, I will! I promise!"

"And don't forget, it must be returned promptly Saturday morning."

As Jessica took the elaborate box in her hands, she thought she'd faint. The box alone probably cost more than most people's houses.

"Come with me," he said with a wave of his arm. "I need for you to sign a few important papers, and then it's all yours."

Elizabeth couldn't help but laugh at her sister. Only a moment ago Jessica had been melodramatically portraying a sophisticated film star for Mr. Donantelli's benefit. Now as she charged across the maroon carpet toward Elizabeth, she was dancing around like a little kid.

Waving the Donantelli jewel case over her head,

Jessica looped her arm through Elizabeth's, locking elbows and spinning her around. "Now, aren't you glad we came?"

"Yes, I am," Elizabeth said with a laugh. Jessica's happiness was so contagious, Elizabeth almost felt like dancing with her. But instead she pulled her arm free and opened the door for Jessica to dance through. Elizabeth had never been able to show the kind of spontaneous exuberance that was her twin's trademark, but she was satisfied in her own way. Helping Jessica had definitely turned out to be a day maker, even though it meant skipping her meeting with William—

Suddenly an image of William waiting in the shadowy basement stacks came to mind. Elizabeth felt as if a bucket of cold water had been dashed into her face. Well, it wasn't as if she'd promised she'd meet him. He'd only just left the note! For all he knew, she hadn't even received it yet. Still, he probably expected her to be there. Maybe he'd watched to make sure she got the note, even. And William could be so . . .

So *what*?

Elizabeth's emotions sank. She wondered if she'd done the right thing after all.

Just as she and Jessica stepped through the arched doorway of Donantelli's into the center mall walk, Elizabeth saw a blur out of the corner of her eye. She was certain that someone had just ducked behind a huge potted fig tree.

Elizabeth caught her breath. Was William stalking her again? Had he gotten so angry that he'd come to the mall after her? She gulped for air. Maybe she was just being paranoid.

Turning her back on the shadowy figure, she nudged Jessica onward.

"Hey, watch out," Jessica complained. "You almost made me drop my new necklace."

"Sorry," Elizabeth apologized. But she continued to pick up the pace.

"What's the big rush?"

"I told you, I have a lot of things to do."

"OK. OK . . ."

Elizabeth had gone several feet before she realized Jessica was no longer beside her. She looked back to find her sister mesmerized in front of the Gap's wide display window.

Jessica pointed excitedly. "Come here. You've got to see this sweater! I've looked everywhere for something in that shade of green."

"Forget it, Jess. Your budget is way overextended as it is." Elizabeth joined Jessica in front of the window.

"I know, but I was thinking maybe *you* could buy it and I could borrow it."

Elizabeth opened her mouth to argue, but a reflection in the window distracted her. Behind them a tall guy had just ducked behind a center stall of T-shirts.

Someone *was* following them.

"You'll have to come back for the sweater another time," Elizabeth said, taking her sister's arm. "We don't have time for any more shopping today."

Elizabeth took off at a pace somewhere between a walk and a jog. Jessica trailed behind her, complaining with every step. Each time they passed a window, Elizabeth glanced sideways into it. In each window she caught sight of the shadowy reflection following them.

A few feet from the escalator she stopped. If William really was following her, wouldn't it be better to confront him here, where there were throngs of shoppers all around? Letting him follow her and Jessica to the isolated parking garage would only be asking for trouble.

Elizabeth glanced over her shoulder in time to see the figure drop to a bench and bury his face in a newspaper. Indignant fury overpowered her good sense. She shoved her purse into Jessica's arms. "Wait here. I'll be right back."

She charged up to the bench and snatched the newspaper away. "Why are you—" Seeing the blushing face behind the paper caused her to practically choke on her question. "Tom! What do you think you're doing?"

Tom looked around sheepishly. "I—I was just reading the—"

"You were not!" Elizabeth's vision blurred red. "You were following me!"

"Well . . . *you* said you wanted to sit alone in your room and *think!*"

"What if I did? That doesn't give you the right to come chasing after me. Do I have to ask your permission now if I want to go to the mall with my sister?"

Tom stood up and towered over her. "That depends on what you're going to do there."

"Wh-What?" she stammered. She stepped back. "It depends on no such thing! I am a free woman. I can come and go when and where I please!"

"And dress however you please too, huh?"

"Exactly!"

Elizabeth jumped as Jessica nudged her from behind.

"Hey." Jessica twirled Elizabeth's purse by the strap. "If you two are going to be arguing long, I'm going to run back to the Gap and—"

"You go ahead, Jessica," Tom said, as if it were his decision to make. "I'll drive Elizabeth back to campus."

"No, Jess . . ."

But Jessica had already taken off. "It'll only take me a second," she called over her shoulder.

"Back to campus?" Tom asked. "That *is* where you were going, isn't it?"

"None of your business," she snapped. She was so mad, she couldn't decide whether to cry or scream or just smack him.

"If you think I'm taking you to meet—"

"You aren't taking me anywhere!" she cried, clenching her fists at her sides.

"Oh yes, I am!" He stepped very close and lowered his voice. "We've made enough of a scene for now. We are going to calmly take that escalator down to the parking garage. And then you are going to quietly get into my car. I think we need to talk."

"And *I* think you need to leave me alone!" She took off toward the Gap.

She could hear Tom's tennis shoes thudding behind her. He was so close that when she whirled around to confront him again, they were practically toe to toe. "Let me make this as clear as possible, OK? I'm. Not. Going. *Anywhere!* With. You. Got it?"

"No, Liz. I don't 'got it.' What's your problem these days?"

"*My* problem these days? My problem is, I don't know what *your* problem is these days! Have you ever heard of trust? Are you so desperate that you can't let me out of your sight for a moment?" She stomped her foot and waved her finger in his face. "Stop following me!"

Tom clamped his hand over hers. His mouth opened and shut several times before any sound came out. "But Elizabeth, I—"

Elizabeth yanked her hand free. "I have enough on my mind right now without having to worry about you creeping around in the shadows." She spun around just in time to see Jessica emerge from the Gap. In addition to the Donantelli jewelry case, she was carrying Elizabeth's purse and a Gap sack.

"Come on, Jess, let's get back to the dorm! Apparently we have no right of privacy around here." She turned back to take one last look at Tom's scarlet face. "I hope you know, Tom—stalking is a crime in this state."

Grabbing Jessica by the arm, she hurried toward the parking garage.

William grasped a pillow and hugged it to his chest. "What should I do, Dr. Denby?"

"Don't whine, William. It's entirely unbecoming and futile." Dr. Denby let William stew in silence for a moment before speaking again. "I warned you that Elizabeth might not show up for your impromptu date."

"I know you did." William dropped the pillow and snatched up Dr. Denby's Rubik's Cube. Immediately he began to twist the rows of colors. He wasn't interested in solving the puzzle, not really. He just liked having something to do with his hands. And the constant click, click, click of the cube rows seemed reassuring somehow. "I believe I'm dealing with my disappointment quite well. Don't you?"

"If you're entirely certain that you aren't angry with her. You know what harm repressed anger can do."

"I'm not repressing anything." Two sides of the puzzle lined up perfectly. "I *was* angry . . . at first. But I'm not now. I've forgiven Elizabeth completely." He set the cube down beside the couch. "I'm sure she had a very good reason for not meeting me in the library."

"Good. I think you're making remarkable progress."

"I'm making progress with my temper, but what about my progress with Elizabeth? What should I do next? Should I go see her, or should I keep my distance like she demanded in the library?" William nervously cracked his knuckles one by one. "I've stayed away so far, but it's not easy. I want to see her so badly, I can't stand it."

"Why do you think she demanded that you keep away from her?"

"I think because she was frightened of me."

When Dr. Denby remained silent and unmoving, William continued. "But she may not want me to stay away from her now that she knows I'm trustworthy."

"Are you sure she knows?"

"I *think* she does. . . . Well . . ." William's voice faded off as doubt filled his mind. "She will soon."

"You mustn't scare her away. Your Elizabeth has been through a lot in her short years. You will have to approach her delicately. Be casual about it."

"But how?"

"What if you were to accidentally run into her on campus somewhere?"

"Oh, right, like she wouldn't think that was suspicious. You're forgetting, Dr. Denby, Elizabeth is way too smart to fall for anything as blatantly obvious as that. She knows I'm not enrolled at SVU. I have no business lurking around on campus. She'd realize in a second that I was there for one reason and one reason only—to see her. Then she'd think I was stalking her, and we'd be right back where we started, with her running away scared."

"William, use your head. People with IQs far inferior to yours come up with probable excuses all the time. Perhaps an errand might take you there?"

"To her dorm? Right!" he said sarcastically.

But Dr. Denby remained as calm and rational as always. "A more neutral spot might be better. Surely you could think of an errand that might take you across, let's say, the quad."

"The quad?" William closed his eyes and considered the idea. He began to wring his hands nervously. "I don't want to go out on the quad where just anybody could see me." William jumped up and began to pace the room. "I'm not ready for that, Dr. Denby. I can't risk it yet." He turned off the light, plunging the small room into darkness.

Dr. Denby didn't protest. He continued to advise calmly. "You've already risked it. You were there Sunday when you spoke to Elizabeth."

"Yes, but I stayed in the shadows. And even then I was terrified that someone would see me."

"What are you afraid of?"

William lit a candle and carried it to the mirror hanging above the bookshelf. He glared at his misshapen face. "That's an asinine question, Dr. Denby. What do you think? I'm afraid of showing this! What if people laugh at me? What if they run from me like I'm the monster from a slasher movie?"

"You are going to have to face these fears sooner or later. We've talked about them before. If you want Elizabeth to love you, you've got to be brave. You can't hide in the darkness forever."

William crossed back to the couch, sank heavily onto its cushions, and covered his scarred cheek with a small pillow. "But how can I bring *this* into the light?"

"The light is not your enemy, William. Fear is. Light is where life is. You have to be brave and bring your love for Elizabeth into the light if you have any hope it is to flourish. Love is a living thing, like a flower. It needs light to grow."

William's backbone straightened and he dropped the pillow. The very thought of his love for

Elizabeth growing and flourishing like Grandmother's wildflowers suddenly filled him with new hope and courage.

"I'll do it," he decided. "I'll go to the quad. For Elizabeth, I can face anything."

Chapter Eight

"Unbelievable." Elizabeth stewed angrily as she trudged up the grassy embankment behind the English building. With each step her head dropped lower and her arms swung higher.

"Slow down! We're not running a race here," Jessica called from a couple of steps behind her.

"I can't believe we ran out of gas!" Elizabeth snarled.

"At least we were back on campus when the Jeep quit. A stroll across the quad is lots better than being stuck on the freeway."

"You drove the Jeep last," Elizabeth scolded. "You should have put gas in it. That's the rule of sharing. If you empty the tank, you're supposed to fill it back up!"

"I didn't drive it last," Jessica argued. "You did."

Elizabeth made a growl of exasperation.

"Driving you back to the mall today doesn't count!"

"Whatever," Jessica said. "But let's not argue about it now. I don't want to spoil my mood. I'm too excited about my necklace." She patted the case lovingly. "You can always get some gas for the Jeep later."

Elizabeth skidded to a halt and threw up her hands. "Oh no, I won't! Why do *I* always have to be the one to fill the tank? Anyway, whatever happened to all those promises you made?"

Jessica looked at her as if she were speaking a foreign language.

Elizabeth pulled the jewelry case from her sister's hand. "Correct me if I'm wrong, but I seem to recall someone who looked just like you promising me the world if only I'd go to the mall with her and help her get this precious necklace. Do you have any idea who that might have been?"

"Well, it *could* have been me, but . . ."

Elizabeth cleared her throat loudly and waved the case in front of her sister's eyes.

Jessica snatched the case back again. "OK, it *was* me, but I thought I agreed to take out the trash or something."

"Jes-si-ca!"

"OK, OK." Jessica sighed dramatically. "What do you want?"

"What I *want* is to have our Jeep filled with gas

and parked behind Dickenson Hall where it's supposed to be—preferably before we get a parking ticket."

"And then we'll be even?" Jessica asked brightly.

Elizabeth rolled her eyes. As many messes as she'd bailed Jessica out of, they'd never be even, not if Jessica filled the Jeep's tank every day for a year. But Elizabeth had never kept score before, and she didn't see any reason to start now. "All even," she agreed.

"OK, I'll take care of it later. It's no big deal, really." Jessica skipped a few steps ahead and then turned around and snapped her fingers as if she'd suddenly been reminded of something. "Oh—can I borrow some money for the gas? My new formal sort of wiped out my account. I'll pay you back, though, I promise."

"You're hopeless!" Elizabeth said with a laugh. She could never stay mad at Jessica for long. Jessica would never change. And truthfully, Elizabeth didn't really want her to. Jessica was Jessica, and she loved her—faults and all.

Besides, she couldn't help but feel a little bit guilty about the Jeep running out of gas. There was no doubt that Jessica should have filled it, but Elizabeth *had* just driven home from the mall. She was usually the responsible twin. She should have noticed on the way home that the gas gauge was on *E*. Probably would have—if she hadn't been so

143

furious at Tom Watts. It was all his fault!

"Hey," Jessica said, breaking into her thoughts. "Quit looking so gloomy. I said I'd take care of the Jeep, and I meant it. You should be happy for me. I have the necklace of my dreams—without spending a penny. Can you just imagine what it's going to look like with my new dress? Oh! You haven't even seen my new dress yet. You're going to love it. Lila thinks I was crazy to go with the royal purple, but I think purple can be just as elegant as black, especially with my necklace." She hugged the velvet jewelry case against her chest long enough to suck in enough oxygen to continue. "Lila is going to be positively green when she sees this. She thinks she's so . . ."

Elizabeth paused beneath a tree and crooked her head to one side. Over Jessica's patter she thought she heard her name being called. "Wait just a second, Jess," she interrupted. She glanced around the quad, trying to determine where the sound was coming from.

At first she didn't see anyone familiar, but then she noticed a figure standing in the shadow of the library. She thought it was William but had to look twice to be sure. He was dressed in faded jeans and a pale blue pullover—the exact color of his eyes. She'd never seen him in anything except dark, depressing black.

"Elizabeth!" he called again, and waved.

"Why are you stopping?" Jessica asked. "I

thought you were in such a big hurry. You've been walking like we were going to a fire sale since we left the Jeep. Now—" Jessica's words broke off as Elizabeth returned William's wave. "Who's that?"

"It's William," Elizabeth whispered.

Jessica's mouth dropped open and she gasped. "Ohmigod! *That's* William White? What's that on the side of his face?"

"Shhh—Jessica!" Elizabeth scolded. "I warned you that he was scarred from the accident."

"Yeah, but you didn't tell me he looked worse than that guy in *Phantom of the Opera*."

As William jogged up to meet them, Elizabeth found herself strangely glad to see him. After all, *he* hadn't been the one stalking her through the mall.

"I just got back from shopping at the campus store," William said, holding up a plastic bag emblazoned with the school logo.

"Hmmm," Jessica muttered. "I thought they'd stopped using that logo a long time ago. I haven't seen one of those bags since orientation week."

William shrugged. "I guess they're trying to use up their old supply. Anyway, I cleaned out their entire stock of perfumed candles. Hey, maybe you two can help me decide which scent is best." He opened the bag and peered inside. "I've got gardenia, sunflower, wild roses, peach blossom, and apple blossom."

"Why don't you burn them all at once and say it's a big ol' flower garden," Jessica joked nervously.

"Speaking of flowers," Elizabeth began, hoping to distract William away from Jessica's gawking, "I found your bouquet this morning. Thank you so much."

"And the note?"

"Yes. I got that too. Your poem was very . . . touching." Elizabeth could feel her cheeks growing warm. "I'm sorry I couldn't meet you, but it *was* short notice. I hope you understand. Jessica needed me to help her with a very important errand."

She pulled Jessica, who'd been practically cowering behind her, a step forward.

"Hello, Jessica. You look as radiant as ever. You're so glowing, you make me wish I'd worn my sunglasses."

Jessica giggled, but Elizabeth could tell she was still uneasy about William's appearance. She elbowed her slightly to get her attention away from William's face and tapped on the jewel case.

Exasperated that her sister still continued to stare, Elizabeth added, "We've been at the mall, getting Jessica decked out for a special date. She's going to be attending the IM Awards this Friday with Charles Sampson."

"No kidding!" William seemed to be rapt with interest.

"Show William the necklace you're going to wear," Elizabeth suggested.

Jessica wordlessly opened the box and held it toward William at arm's length.

William didn't seem to take offense at all. He lifted the pearl necklace in his long, slender fingers. "This diamond clasp is breathtaking, Jessica. And the pearls are exquisite. Just look! They have a marvelous, slight pinkish tone that's found in only the very best pearls."

As Jessica nodded happily, he continued, "I can tell you know quality jewelry. I'd say this is a one-of-a-kind creation."

"It is," Jessica agreed, obviously warming to his flattery. "I got it from R. Donantelli's."

"Wise choice! Donantelli's handles only the very best gems. And you don't have to worry about someone next to you wearing the very same necklace. Every piece in his store is an original."

Elizabeth noticed that William seemed to be purposefully keeping his left side to Jessica as he talked. Between that and the barrage of compliments, Jessica seemed much less nervous.

"But you'd better be careful," he said, slipping the necklace back onto its bed of maroon velvet and snapping the lid shut. "The clasp on this box is loose."

"Is it? I'm surprised Mr. Donantelli would give us a broken case." Jessica took the box from William's left hand and examined the latch. "Oh, well, it's just a little bit wobbly. It's no big deal. The necklace is the important thing, not the box. Soon it'll be safely around my neck."

"Where it belongs," William said with a smile. "Only a neck like yours could ever do this necklace justice. I can see why your sister would stand me up. Fetching this treasure was definitely an important mission."

Elizabeth stepped closer to William while Jessica looked lovingly at the necklace. "Thanks for understanding," she whispered.

"No problem," he said with a nonchalant shrug. "I'm cool with it. I knew when I sent you the note that I wasn't giving you a lot of notice. But you can't blame a guy for taking a chance."

"You aren't mad?"

William smiled as if he'd expected her to ask that very question. "No. I was disappointed, of course, but I figured . . . some other time."

Elizabeth noticed that William turned his whole face toward her as he spoke. She felt oddly proud that he seemed confident enough in her to reveal what was evidently very painful for him.

"If that's OK with you, that is," he added quietly.

"Of course. Some other time," she agreed. When she first said the words, she was only being polite, but once the sentence was out in the open, she was very glad she'd said it. William looked elated as he hurried back across the quad and disappeared into the shady walkway that ran around the south side of the library. William was something else, all right. He was so polite, so respectful, and so understanding . . . unlike Tom Watts.

"I can't believe that was William White!" Jessica said as Dickenson Hall came into view.

"Jess, don't be so judgmental. Just because he has a few scars—"

"I wasn't talking about that. 'Cause really, if you don't look at his bad side, he's still as gorgeous as ever. I just meant because he acts so different. He's nothing like William the psycho. More like the old suave, smooth William, the one you had the hots for when we first got here."

"Jessica, I did not have—"

Jessica ignored Elizabeth's pathetic denial and kept talking. "Do you think he's on some miracle mood-altering drug or something?"

"No . . . I think it's his face."

"Get real," Jessica said. For a brainiac Elizabeth's thinking could be so convoluted sometimes.

"I'm serious," Elizabeth insisted. "I think that maybe being scarred has taken away some of his egotistical 'I'm perfect' attitude. You know how he was. He spent his whole life thinking he was superior to every living creature. But now I think the scarring has not only brought him down a peg, but has made him look into himself. He's

149

realized the way he was treating everyone else. Poor guy. I feel sorry for him."

Jessica yawned. "Thanks, Dr. Freud, for telling me five times more than I wanted to know. I was just wondering why you didn't tell me you two had a date."

"We didn't. Not really. He just sent me flowers and a note asking me to meet him in the library."

Jessica could vaguely remember there being a lot of flowers lying about their room, but she hadn't given them much notice. Why care about a bunch of silly flowers when she had Charles Sampson, Donantelli jewelry, a magnificent dress, and the IM Awards on her mind? "Well, I wouldn't consider a meeting in the library a *date*," Jessica began, "but it sure sounds like your typical night of fun."

Elizabeth gave her a snotty-big-sister look.

"So, are you going to see him again?"

"I don't know if I should . . . you know, because of . . . things."

"What things?"

"Jessica! We're talking about *William White*." Elizabeth tapped the side of her head. "Remember Todd being thrown in jail? Or our friends careening down a mountain road in a van without brakes?"

"Here we go again. I think you need to relax a little. You're the one who's always saying give people the benefit of the doubt. Forgive and forget and all that."

150

"Some things you can't forget—or forgive."

"Well, I don't know. William seems fine to me." Jessica smiled, remembering all the nice things he'd said about her necklace and about her skill at appreciating fine jewelry. He couldn't be all that bad. "In fact, I think he's a real gentleman, something sorely lacking around campus these days. I think you should consider going out with him."

"Right! Me and half the Sweet Valley police force, maybe." Elizabeth sighed. "Besides, what makes you think he's going to ask me out?"

"Oh, he'll ask, all right. He's got it bad for you."

"You think?"

"Well, duh? I think that's way obvious, sister dear. For a straight-A student, you're pretty dense." Tired of discussing her sister's boring love life, Jessica opened the case and peeked at the beautiful necklace again. "I think I'll take this over to Theta house and show Lila."

"Absolutely not!"

"But I want to show it to everybody!"

"No way! We're already at the dorm, and we're going to take it upstairs where it'll be safe."

"It's perfectly safe with me," Jessica insisted.

"Listen, Jess. If everyone sees it before the ceremony, it won't have the same impact. Why don't you just describe it to them and tell them they'll have to watch you on TV if they want to see it for real?"

Jessica chewed thoughtfully on a fingernail. For once Elizabeth might actually have a good fashion-related point. She could go over to the sorority house tonight and brag all she wanted. She'd still get plenty of attention. And then Friday night they'd all be glued to the TV. It'd be like double time in the spotlight, and she'd be in Smug City.

"You're right, Liz," Jessica admitted grandly. "I'm not going to let a soul see the necklace until it's on my neck." *Except, maybe . . . Lila,* she silently added.

Chapter
Nine

"Oh, Jessica," Elizabeth grumbled as she tripped over a pair of boots in the middle of the floor. She tossed them toward Jessica's side of the room and didn't bother to watch where they landed. The entire place was a disaster area anyway. Jessica had promised to clear up the debris from her latest closet excavation, but so far she hadn't found the time.

"Well, I might as well just count my blessings," Elizabeth reminded herself. At least the Jeep was full of gas and back in the parking lot where it belonged. Even if Jessica *had* conned Winston Egbert into retrieving the Jeep and Elizabeth into paying for the gas.

Elizabeth glanced at the alarm clock beside her bed. It was nearly eleven o'clock, and she was exhausted—mentally and physically. She decided to forget about Tom Watts, forget homework, forget everything, and go to bed early for once.

There was no sense waiting up for Jessica; no telling how late she'd stay at Theta house. She'd probably be there as long as one of her sorority sisters would stay awake listening to her brag about her exciting date, her glamorous formal, and her spectacular necklace.

Elizabeth smiled indulgently at the thought of her sister's tendency to exaggerate. But all exaggeration aside, Elizabeth had to admit, it *was* a gorgeous necklace.

She looked over at where the maroon case lay on Jessica's desk, right next to her makeup mirror—a place of honor and the cleanest spot on Jessica's side of the room. Maybe Elizabeth was being silly, but she felt uncomfortable having something so expensive lying around the dorm room. If anyone knew it was up here, it'd be child's play to break into the dorm and steal it. And any number of people could have seen them bring it home. After all, the mall had been crowded. Any of the shoppers could have been a thief in disguise. They could have seen Jessica waving the necklace around and simply followed their Jeep back to campus. All they would have had to do was wait until the lights went out. . . .

They could be waiting outside the dorm right this very second. Waiting for our lights to go off, thinking that means it's all clear to break in . . .

"You've been watching too many bad movies, Wakefield," Elizabeth told herself.

She pulled the scrunchie from her ponytail and shook loose her hair. Then, in her old cutoff sweats and SVH T-shirt, she flopped back on her bed and clicked off her light. Just as she began to sink into sleep, she heard a pinging rap against the window.

She bolted upright. All her senses shut down automatically except for her hearing. Her ears pricked up and honed in like radar.

Whack!

There it was again. Something definitely had been thrown against the glass. Without turning on the light, she tiptoed over to the window and drew back the curtain.

Someone stood in the narrow, grassy area beneath her window, just in a spot where the lights from the parking lot didn't shine. She peered harder at the shadowy apparition. Then it moved, and she caught a flash of white blond hair. It was William! And he seemed to be yelling something up at her window.

She opened the window and leaned out.

Far below her, William clasped his hands in a pleading gesture like Romeo in the famous balcony scene. "Elizabeth. Can I come up?"

"I guess so," she replied, still half asleep. She wondered why he hadn't just come up and knocked on her door. She had no doubt that he knew the way. He'd been there often enough in the past, leaving things. Notes and mutilated Barbie dolls . . .

Elizabeth was suddenly not so sure she wanted to be alone with him. Why had she rashly invited him up? She was practically asleep, that's why.

She opened her mouth to cancel the invitation, but her sleepy brain couldn't come up with a good excuse. And anyway, maybe she was being unfair. He hadn't done anything wrong—lately. He wasn't skulking and sneaking around like the new, *un*improved Tom Watts. He was openly asking if he could come up.

William pointed toward the dark steel door of the rear emergency exit. "Would you come let me in the back way? There's no door handle."

She almost shouted for him to go around to the front entrance, but it suddenly occurred to her that he was too self-conscious about his appearance to brave the bright, crowded front lobby of Dickenson Hall.

"I'll be right down," she yelled to William. She stepped into her sandals and hurried down the hall. Letting William in the back way was probably a good idea anyway. The way gossip flew around campus, Tom would be banging on her door in a jealous rage before she had time to offer William a seat.

She scurried down the fire stairs and pushed the lever on the emergency door with a loud clang.

"Thanks," William said as he followed Elizabeth up the back stairs. "I didn't know if it'd be OK to come in this way. I figured the door had an alarm on it."

"There used to be one, but it's been disconnected. It was accidentally set off so many times, you know. I bet the administration got tired of paying false-alarm fees to the fire department."

"That's not too cool," William observed.

"I know. Dickenson Council has requested that it be fixed, but . . . well . . . feet tend to shuffle when it comes to these things." Elizabeth paused and waited for William to step up next to her. Maybe it was silly, but she felt uneasy having him behind her.

William hurried ahead and opened the stairwell door for her. The hallway was deserted as they made their way to her room.

"Are you thirsty?" Elizabeth asked as she let him into her room and switched on the overhead light. "I can make us some tea. If you don't mind that I'll have to make it in a hot pot or that we'll have to drink from regular old coffee mugs."

"Tea sounds great. And don't worry about the hot pot. It's been quite a while since I've observed the niceties of a real tea service. I don't have anyone to have tea with anymore, unless you count Dr. Denby. He's . . . taking care of me. Dr. Denby's not really much of a tea drinker. I think he only puts up with it because he knows I enjoy it."

"He sounds like a really nice man."

"Oh, he is. He's a wonderful doctor, Elizabeth. You'd like him. I hope you have a chance to meet him someday. I owe him my life, literally. I'd never have been allowed to improve in that prison hospital. I think they hoped I'd just die and leave an empty bed for someone more deserving."

His tone broke her heart. "Oh, I'm so—"

"I'm sorry," he interrupted. "I wasn't fishing for pity. I didn't mean to bring you down."

Elizabeth wasn't sure how to react. To cover her sudden awkwardness, she busied herself by filling the hot pot with bottled water from the minifridge. She set it on top of the fridge and plugged it in. "Now, where did I put those tea bags?"

"I see Jessica hasn't changed her decor," William said, walking aimlessly around the tiny dorm room while Elizabeth rummaged through the large plastic container where she and Jessica kept their snack supplies.

He picked up a magazine, glanced at the cover, and set it back down on Jessica's bed. "She's still an avid movie fan, I see."

"Worse than ever—especially now that she has that invitation to the IM Awards." Elizabeth found the tea bags and held them up victoriously. "Ta da! And look. I've even found us some cookies."

"Terrific. But don't go to a lot of trouble for

me. I just wanted to drop by and see you."

Elizabeth unwrapped the tea bags and arranged a half-dozen cookies on a plate. When she looked up again, William was standing beside Jessica's desk, as if frozen there. At first she wondered what he was looking at, but then it dawned on her with embarrassment that he was staring at his own face in Jessica's ever present makeup mirror. It had to be hard to constantly have that scarred, masklike stranger staring back at him. She wondered if he ever got used to it, but didn't dare ask.

"Tea's almost ready," she announced.

"Need any help?"

"You can scoot Jessica's desk chair over by mine near the window."

"What shall I do with these things?" he asked, holding up a pile of magazines.

"Just dump them anywhere. On her desk if you can find a spot, or just use the floor if you can't. She'll never know the difference."

"Anything else?"

"There's a TV tray folded behind my desk that we use for a little table. You could get that out."

While Elizabeth poured hot water into ceramic mugs, she could hear William arranging a place for them.

"Milk?" she asked, carrying the mugs over to the TV tray and setting them down.

"Just sugar if you have it."

Elizabeth settled into Jessica's desk chair and scooted it up to the TV tray. William sat across from her, hunched over his mug. He looked uncomfortable, and for some reason that made her feel uncomfortable as well.

"Is it too hot in here for you? You could take your jacket off and—"

"No. I'm not too warm." He shifted in her desk chair and pulled his jacket more tightly around him. "Actually . . . it's that overhead light. Would you mind terribly if we turned it off?"

Elizabeth hesitated, suddenly nervous. What did William have in mind? What if she said no?

William cupped one hand over his eyebrow. "I hate to be a bother, but direct light hurts my injured eye."

His request seemed reasonable enough. Relieved, Elizabeth set down her mug and wiped her moist hands on the legs of her jeans. "You should have said something earlier." She turned on her desk lamp and switched off the brighter overhead light. "Is that better?"

"Much, but would you mind if I move the shade down just a little?"

"Go ahead," she said with a shrug. "Adjust it however it's comfortable for you."

William leaned across her desk and tilted the shade slightly. "Hey," he said, picking up a paper from where Elizabeth had been working earlier that evening. "What's this?"

"It's a list of items I'm cataloging for the library-archives committee."

"I've heard a little about that." William's good eye scanned down the page. "It looks interesting. Where'd you find all this stuff?"

As Elizabeth filled him in about the archives project, William sat with rapt attention. It felt good to be able to talk about something that interested her for once. She'd almost forgotten what it was like to have a two-sided conversation, where the other party actually responded with intelligent comments. Lately Tom's end of any conversation was hardly more than an occasional polite "uh-huh." Unless he was talking about *his* interests, of course. Then he could go on and on ad nauseam. But any topic other than WSVU bored him after about ten seconds. Maybe he'd always been that way and she'd just never noticed. But ever since she'd left the TV station, he didn't seem to care about what she was doing.

Her thoughts suddenly left her feeling guilty again. Tom was just one more reason she shouldn't have let William come up to her room. Trying to distance herself from him, she reached for her mug and took a sip of tea.

"Have you come across any census records or deeds that mention Sweet Valley?" he asked, looking up from her notes.

She swallowed her bite of cookie and wiped her mouth. "Actually, I came across a couple today. They're listed on another sheet. Here—let me get it." Elizabeth leaned across to her desk and easily located the paper she wanted. She scooted her mug to one side and laid the list on the TV tray. "Can you see all right, or do you need more light?"

"I'm afraid I can't see as well as I used to." William scooted his chair closer to hers. "But I'm fine if I get close enough to what I'm trying to read."

"Let me show you some of the things I've found."

As they leaned together over the list, William's handsome left side was all she could see. Suddenly she shivered. She was being drawn to him like a magnet to steel, just the way she'd been when they had first met, and now, just like then, she couldn't stop herself. He was so refined and fascinating . . . so polite and . . . and . . . appealing. He was everything Tom wasn't. Smooth, wealthy, brilliant . . . and he smelled so inviting.

William leaned closer. Elizabeth closed her eyes and enjoyed the sensation of William's warm breath tickling against her cheek . . . her neck. She was like a cold, shivering creature being invited into a soft, warm cocoon. His hand accidentally brushed hers, and her heart fluttered nervously.

"Elizabeth," he whispered, leaning even closer.

Moistening her lips, she waited expectantly for his kiss.

Tom bit another antacid tablet and stuck the roll back in his pocket. His stomach was a big, churning acid pit, and it was all Elizabeth's fault. Determined to confront her with his feelings, he stalked across the dark campus in rapid, long-legged strides.

Ever since returning from the mall, his night had been a total loss. None of his attempts to get his mind off their fight had worked. He hadn't been able to study. He'd been a tyrant at the television studio. And he'd even gotten into a senseless argument with his roommate, Danny Wyatt. He couldn't let this go on any longer.

What had gotten into Elizabeth this afternoon? Well, perhaps he'd been wrong to follow her. And once again he should have tried harder to keep his raging temper in check. But she shouldn't have gone off on him the way she had. "We're going to talk this out once and for all," he vowed under his breath. "She's going to have to see reason eventually."

What if she's already gone to bed? he wondered, hearing the big campus clock in the quad chime eleven. Oh, well. If she had, he wasn't going to let

163

that stop him. He'd just have to wake her. It was time to clear up a few issues between them right now.

Cutting across Dickenson Hall's rear parking lot, he paused and scanned across the back side of the familiar cinder-block building to the second row of windows. He counted four across. Elizabeth's window glowed brightly. "Good," he muttered. "She's still awake."

Suddenly he tensed like a setter on point. There were *two* people in that room.

Squinting in disbelief, he easily picked out Elizabeth's shape silhouetted against the shade, but the other shadow was much too brawny to be Jessica's. And they were much too close together. "It's . . . a guy!" he growled. "I knew she was seeing someone else!"

The realization hit Tom like a karate kick to the gut. He fumbled for his pack of antacids again. They fell from his fingers. He heard them clunk to the asphalt, but he couldn't take his eyes off the window.

As painful as it was to watch, he couldn't peel his eyes away as the two shadowy heads leaned closer and closer. When Tom could no longer see light between them, his heart kicked into hyperspeed and his breathing stopped. Overcome with jealousy, he ran as fast as he could toward the dorm's main entrance.

*   *   *

The hairs on Elizabeth's arms began to prickle, and she shivered. This was exactly the same sensation she'd felt in her CyberDreams. Hot, cold. Attraction, repulsion. Desire and fear were mixed together, and she felt as if her brain were short-circuiting, but there was nothing she could do. She shuddered. Every CyberDream had ended the same way—in disaster!

She shifted away from William so suddenly, he must have thought she was falling. He wrapped an arm around her shoulder.

"What's wrong, Elizabeth?" he asked in surprise. "If I did or said something wrong, I'm sorry."

"No. I'm just . . ." Her voice drifted off as she flashed back to standing in that vast, creepy cyberlibrary with its endless rows and rows of shadow-casting file cabinets. She could almost feel the darkness closing in around her and a murderous William appearing from nowhere. The very memory filled her with a hollow, scary feeling that completely erased any romantic notions she'd had just moments ago. She sighed and unwound herself from William's arm. "I'm just tired."

"Oh, wow. How thoughtless of me." His spine straightened. He seemed taller, more threatening for a second.

Elizabeth scooted farther away and climbed to her feet.

"I'm really embarrassed," William said, rising to his feet beside her. "It was already late when I came over, and now I've overstayed my welcome. I didn't mean to take up so much of your time, but I got so interested in that stuff about the library, I just lost track. You must think I'm a selfish creep."

"No. I—I had a good time," she said. "But if you wouldn't mind going now, I just—I don't feel very well. Maybe we can talk again . . . some other time."

"Just name the time and place. I'm always happy to see you, Elizabeth. You know that."

"Soon," she said evasively. She felt so confused, she honestly didn't know what to say. "Thanks for being so understanding."

"No problem," he said as she opened the door into the hallway. "Will the back door be locked if I leave by the fire stairs?"

"No, it can always be opened from the inside. There's just no latch on the outside."

Elizabeth closed the door behind William and leaned against it. Her head was swimming with conflicting emotions. She didn't know what to feel. Fear? Guilt? Anger? Caution? Hate? Pity? Love?

No, not love! I'm going crazy!

She *had* to be crazy to have let William in her room when she was all alone. She had no proof that he'd changed. OK, so he'd acted like a perfect gentleman. That didn't mean much. William had proved many times before that he could be as charming and well mannered as a Romeo and Don Juan combined and still have murder on his mind.

And I was even thinking about kissing him!

"No, I wasn't," she argued with herself. Why would she want to kiss William when she was in love with Tom?

"Oh, who am I trying to kid," she mumbled. She really *had* wanted William to kiss her, tenderly and passionately. But if that was true, what about Tom? Was she just bored for the moment? Or had she actually fallen out of love with him?

Tom banged on Elizabeth's door, not caring if he was loud enough to wake half the dorm. "Elizabeth, open up!"

"Tom?" She opened the door sooner than he expected, causing him to stumble forward slightly. "What are you doing here?"

Her expression was all wide-eyed surprise, but he didn't believe it for a second. She'd answered the door so quickly, it was almost as if she'd been standing behind it, waiting for him.

"Where is he?" Tom shouted.

Elizabeth's eyebrows knitted together in confusion. Her hair was loose, falling around her face in golden waves. It'd been ages since she'd worn her hair that way for him.

"Don't give me that innocent look. I know you've got a guy in here!" Tom shouldered his way around her and into the room.

Elizabeth's desk light was on, but the rest of the room was dim and shadowy. He noted two ceramic mugs on a TV tray near the window. That's where he'd seen them—together. Kissing!

He turned toward her bed. Seeing that the covers were all rumpled caused a knot in his stomach the size of a football. He slammed his fist into her pillow.

"There's nobody here but me, Tom. And how dare you barge in on me this way?"

Tom tuned her out. He spun around in the middle of the room—fists up, ready to fight. "There you are, you pathetic coward!" he snarled as he dived for the suspicious lump in the middle of Jessica's bed. He yanked the purple comforter to the floor, sending pillows, magazines, and clothes flying across the room.

"Tom! Stop it!"

"He's in the closet, isn't he?" Tom jerked the closet door open and rammed his fists into Elizabeth's neatly hanging clothes.

Elizabeth pulled him away from her closet and toward the exit, but Tom yanked free and turned toward Jessica's closet. Although the door was already standing wide open, Tom didn't bother looking there. No human being could have squeezed into the tiny space left from her mess.

He again scanned the room. There was nowhere else to hide, except possibly under Elizabeth's bed; Jessica's was as messy as her closet. Tom dropped to his knees.

"Stop it, Tom! So help me, if you look under that bed, I'm calling security."

She *was* hiding someone! Tom lowered his head and shoved aside the dust ruffle.

"That does it!" Elizabeth scrambled around him and grabbed the phone. "You're out of control."

"Wait!" he shouted, climbing to his feet. "I'm calming down. Don't call security." He held out his hands in a pleading gesture.

Elizabeth replaced the receiver but kept one hand on top of the phone. "Tom, I'm tired of your jealousy. You have no right to come in here searching my room."

Tom tried to keep his attention on her but couldn't. His gaze continued to bounce from one corner of the room to the next, constantly searching.

"I'm serious," she warned. "Ever since we visited that crazy CyberDreams tent, you haven't given me a moment's peace. I want you to quit spying on me. Quit stalking me, and quit treating me like I'm your prized possession."

"Is that what you think I've been doing?"

"What else am I supposed to think? Every time I turn around, there you are."

"Funny, but I always thought that when two people were in love, they wanted to be together."

"Funny, but *I* always thought that when two people were in love, they trusted each other and respected each other's privacy."

Tom craned his neck to look behind the door. "I know I saw a guy in here."

"Stop it right now and get out!"

Tom couldn't help himself. The thought of Elizabeth being with someone else drove him insane. Ignoring her threats, he looked under Jessica's desk, then under Elizabeth's. Suddenly he stopped short and gasped. The flowers he'd sent Elizabeth lay upside down in the trash.

"I don't believe it!" he howled, pointing to the sagging, crushed bouquet. "Why, Elizabeth?"

She cowered against her desk.

"I think I at least deserve some sort of explanation."

"They were starting to wilt," she said lamely.

"Right! That's probably because those tacky dandelions are soaking up the water in the fancy glass urn meant for *my* arrangement—the urn I paid for, I might add."

"I'm sorry, Tom." But she didn't look sorry.

"Forget it. It's pretty obvious where I stand

with you." Tom stormed toward the door. "If that's the way you feel, I don't know why I keep trying. Just forget it. It's over between us! Tell your new boyfriend he can come out of whatever dark, roachy crevice he's hiding in. 'Cause I'm outta here!"

Chapter
Ten

"Just wait, Li. You are *not* going to believe this necklace even when you see it." Jessica unlocked the door and motioned Lila inside her dorm room.

"I still don't understand why you didn't just bring it with you to Theta house last night," Lila said. "It would have been a lot easier than making me walk all the way over to Dickenson today."

Jessica grinned and brushed some lint from her new green sweater. Elizabeth had been right. Keeping the actual necklace from her friends had been a stroke of genius. Her stories about the necklace had left every Theta drooling to see it—especially Lila.

"Well, where *is* this masterpiece?" Lila asked impatiently. "I have places to go, people to see. . . ." She waved her hand dramatically.

Jessica picked up the maroon jewelry case and waved it under Lila's nose. She was positively loving the sickly green tinge of envy around Lila's gills. And that was just from seeing the box. Jessica stalled to prolong the dramatic effect. Why not let her suffer? Lila deserved it for not helping her yesterday.

"Hurry up! I've seen boxes from Donantelli's before. Let's see the goods." Lila rubbed her hands together greedily.

"You should have seen Raoul when I told him I used to be on *The Young and the Beautiful*. He practically begged me to wear this necklace. He claims it's the most expensive piece he ever created."

"Jessica. Get on with it. Are you going to show me this necklace or not?"

"Of course. Just be patient."

"I'm tired of being patient. I'm beginning to believe there's nothing in that stupid box. You're just making all this up because you're ticked about yesterday. Aren't you?" Lila tried to snatch the jewelry case from Jessica's hands, but Jessica was too quick. "Jessica Wakefield, if you've dragged me all the way over here for nothing, I'm gonna—"

"Ta daa!" Jessica opened the box with a flourish.

Seeing Lila's face sent her into a fit of giggles. Her expression was even more goggle-eyed goofy than Jessica had hoped for.

174

After a couple of seconds of staring into the box, Lila pinched her lips together in a very unbecoming frown and glared. "Ha-ha. Very funny."

"What's funny?"

Lila brushed her long, dark hair out of her face. "Now, if you're through with your immature games, I believe I'll get back to life in the *adult* world."

"What games?" Jessica asked, her amusement dying in her throat.

"I *knew* you didn't have a Donantelli original. I don't know where you got the empty case. I have to admit, it really *looks* like a Donantelli case. You almost had me going there, but—"

Jessica flipped the case around and peered inside. "It's empty!" she squealed. Her pulse began to flutter, and a very unattractive sweat began to pop out along her upper lip. "Where is it?" She ripped her comforter off her bed and shook it. She frantically checked her desk and the floor. Nothing.

"You mean there really was a necklace?"

"Of *course* there was a necklace! Why would I make up something like that? I'd never tell a lie that lame!" Jessica closed the case and let it fall to her bed.

"Jessica, are you telling me you actually, truly had a Raoul Donantelli pearl choker and you've *lost* it?"

"I couldn't have lost it. There's no way!"

Suddenly Jessica's legs turned into rubber bands and wobbled beneath her. She fell to her bed, right next to the case.

"Well, where could it be?" Lila asked.

"If I knew that, I wouldn't be sitting here having a panic attack, now, would I?" Jessica buried her face in her hands. "This can't be happening to me. It can't," she moaned. "Oh, this is the absolute worst! It's gone. I've lost it."

"How could you have lost it?"

"Will you stop asking me dumb questions? I don't know how I could have lost it. Or when. Or where." Jessica lifted the case again and shook it, as if she were hoping Donantelli had given her a trick jewelry box and the pearls would reappear by magic. The case popped open in her hands.

"Oh my gosh. I forgot! The clasp on the case was loose. Maybe the necklace fell out somewhere on campus yesterday when Elizabeth and I walked back to the dorm."

Lila arched an eyebrow. "Wanna bet some lucky college student is one megabunch richer today?"

"Don't joke, Li. I'm in big trouble here. That necklace costs more than my entire college education . . . no. *Two* college educations—mine and Elizabeth's put together. And that's just what it'll cost me if I don't return that necklace first thing Saturday morning! What am I going to do?"

*   *   *

Elizabeth sneezed loudly and grabbed another tissue. Her nose and eyes had been itching like crazy ever since she'd opened that last dusty file cabinet drawer. But despite the dust and the pathetically weak lighting, Elizabeth was enjoying her work. If only she could keep her mind on it.

She couldn't quit thinking about Tom and William. Even though she'd been furious about the way Tom had barged into her room last night, their breakup didn't seem quite real. She knew it had happened. Tom's parting words had been quite clear. But it just didn't feel right. All morning she'd been trying to figure out why she wasn't more upset.

Once, several months ago, she and Tom had a misunderstanding that led to their breaking up. At that time Elizabeth felt as if her whole world had crumbled. She'd cried until she had no more tears. She hadn't been able to eat, or sleep, or concentrate on her class work. She'd been a total basket case. Shouldn't she be falling apart right now?

She bit the end of her pencil and looked at the stack of yellowed papers on the desk in front of her. Papers she'd already cataloged today. She was apparently functioning just fine.

Was she in denial? Was she being calm because she knew she and Tom would eventually get back together when he cooled down? Or could it be that she simply didn't care anymore?

It was hard to feel sad and mad at the same time—and lately, mad was definitely taking precedence. Tom's jealousy and possessiveness had gotten way out of hand. Take, for instance, how he'd followed her and Jessica to the mall yesterday. And then, even worse, he'd gone and stormed through her room last night, practically ransacking the place, looking for evidence that she'd been unfaithful.

She pursed her lips in disgust. If someone had just met both Tom Watts and William White for the first time, Tom would appear to be the psycho one, not William. Tom's temper had always been a problem, but now—it was *beyond*.

And William . . . there was another puzzling situation. If Tom had changed from nice Dr. Jekyll into monstrous Mr. Hyde, it seemed that William had done the exact opposite. William had been a perfect gentleman. Even their near kiss in her room last night had been more her fault than his. She'd been the one conjuring up cyberfantasies. And further proof of his transformation to good guy was in the way he'd reacted when she'd asked him to leave. He couldn't have been more civil and contrite.

Evidently William's psychiatrist was a miracle worker. And Dr. Denby couldn't have done it alone. William had to want to be cured. The very fact that he'd tried so hard to change his evil ways really touched her. Maybe she ought to find out how to hook Tom up with Dr. Denby. He could really use a session or two. Or ten. Or twenty.

With a tired sigh Elizabeth forced her mind back to work. She jotted a note on the bottom of her clipboard and slipped the crumbling quit-claim deeds back into their yellowed envelope. Out beside her note she wrote "1857" and "150 acres." It was about all she'd been able to decipher from the scratchy, loopy handwriting. Digging up the past wasn't as easy as she'd expected.

"There," she announced, adding the envelope to the top of the stack on the desk. "That takes care of another drawer."

Hoisting the awkward stack of papers and files, she shuffled across the room to the file cabinet. Unable to see her feet, she walked cautiously, reminding herself to step over the gas pipe that protruded from the wall just inside the doorway.

Repacking all the envelopes and files back into the cramped wooden cabinet was almost as big a job as cataloging them. Not only did she have to work awkwardly, bent at the waist, but the crazy files seemed to grow thicker when they were freed from their storage drawer. She could only put them back a file or two at a time—firmly pressing each to the front before adding the next few. The work was tediously slow because she had to be careful not to damage the brittle documents.

Finished at last, she looked back at the antique

desk that she'd set up as her temporary workstation and sighed. She needed to stretch the kinks out of her back before tackling another stack of files.

She considered a walk on campus, but that would waste too much of her precious time. She settled instead on walking around the room, swinging her arms and stretching her legs.

After a few laps she stopped to admire the elegant bookcase built into the wall opposite the door. She'd never seen one quite like it. It was slightly raised from the floor by two smooth, wooden steps. The craftsmanship was amazing. It almost looked as if the bookcase and steps were built from a single, enormous piece of dark wood.

She wondered if the steps were supposed to be decorative or functional. From their well-worn appearance, she guessed functional. But why? Was their purpose to keep the books away from the damp floor? Or were they simply an aid for shorter people to reach books on the top shelves? She'd always heard people were shorter back then.

Well, for whatever reason it was designed the way it was, it was still beautiful. She stepped up on the bottom step and laid her hands against the cool, smooth books. How she wished she'd been given the job of cataloging the old books. But she couldn't blame John Petrie for grabbing that job for himself. She could just imagine his excitement if he uncovered some rare first edition. Sometimes rare old books sold at auctions for thousands and thousands of dollars each. It would be amazing to find a treasure like that down in the archives. All that money would mean a lot to the library—or even to the college in general.

She backed her head away slightly so she could read the title of the book right in front of her nose. *Gulliver's Travels . . . how old is this edition?* she wondered. It amazed her to think that someone could have pulled this very book off this very shelf, sat in this very room, and read about Gulliver and the Lilliputians by the light of a flickering gas lamp—or maybe even a candle. That thought suddenly made her appreciate the measly bulb hanging in the doorway.

"Thank goodness for electricity," she whispered. As much as she liked the wondrous feeling that she was touching the past, she didn't want to take it too far. She was pretty dependent on modern conveniences.

"I'd better get back to work," she reminded herself. But as she turned, a large, brightly colored book caught her eye. Even through the dust and cobwebs its golden cover and reddish lettering set it apart. She couldn't help but touch it.

Strange. It wasn't leather bound, like the other books. *What is it made of?* she wondered. *Silk? Some kind of damask?* She glanced over her shoulder as if checking to see if she were alone—knowing full well that she was. No one else had been down in the archives all day. She knew she probably shouldn't bother things, but who'd know if she just took the book off the shelf for a quick peek?

She stepped on the top step and her tiptoes to reach the top edge of the beautiful volume. She had trouble making out the worn letters. *It looks like a* P-U . . . *no, it's an* O. O-L. *Or it could be* P-O-E. *Poe? Omigosh! What if it's a first edition of Edgar Allan Poe's stories?* Her fingers trembled with anticipation as she reached up and pulled on the spine of the book.

She hardly had time to scream and grab on for dear life. The whole bookshelf spun around like some ancient carnival ride, carrying her with it into darkness.

As it jerked to a halt, she gasped, sucking in a lungful of musky, dank air. The darkness around her was so thick, she felt as if a black bag had been pulled over her head. Still clinging to the wooden shelf with one hand, she reached out timidly behind her with the other, feeling nothing but cold emptiness. She fumbled for the yellow book, which still tilted outward over her head, and yanked on it. Nothing happened. She pushed it in and yanked it back out again.

Still nothing.

She was trapped.

*   *   *

Jessica stood up, brushed the grass from her knees, and readjusted her bright red mini.

"Find anything?" Lila asked for about the millionth time.

Jessica shook her head sadly. "Not a pearl. Not a single pearl." She had retraced every step that she and Elizabeth had made across the quad—even going so far as to crawl around in the bushes near the spot where they'd run into William White.

"What were you and Elizabeth doing in the bushes?" Lila asked snidely.

Jessica didn't have the patience left to humor her friend. "We came straight across here," she muttered. "I thought maybe it could have fallen out of the case while we were walking and rolled under these bushes."

"Maybe it just blew away on a breeze," Lila said sarcastically. "Get real, Jess. The way you described that necklace, it must have weighed five pounds. It couldn't just disappear. If you dropped it, then you might as well face the music. It's gone. You're going to have to deal with it."

"Lila, you could be a little bit supportive!" Jessica's lower lip began to quiver, and tears blurred her vision. It was all too much. She quit holding back the tears and let them fall.

"Well, what are you going to do?"

"There's nothing else I *can* do. You're right. The necklace is gone, and I'm dead."

*   *   *

William settled back on the couch and gnawed on his fingernails while he waited for Dr. Denby's comments on his latest confession.

"Worry is good, William. It shows that you're normal. And so is a certain amount of guilt. Just don't go overboard with it."

"Then you think it's OK?" William asked hesitantly. "You don't think I was wrong to do what I did?"

"The word *wrong* has so many connotations. Let's just say, what you did was . . . justifiable."

"You mean, I had a good excuse."

"Something like that."

William leaned forward confidentially. "You don't think what I did was too drastic, do you?"

"Maybe a little, but you wanted to get Elizabeth to trust you, right?"

"Absolutely!"

"Do you think this is going to help?"

"I know it will."

Dr. Denby smiled. "Then I don't think you need to dwell on it anymore. You weren't acting out of anger. There was nothing mean or evil in your action, and no one got hurt. You were simply doing what you had to do in order to make Elizabeth see how you've changed. Right?"

"Right. But do you think I was unfair to her?"

"William, just remember that old saying, 'All's fair in love and war.'"

"And this is love." William sighed happily and

hugged his knees to his chest. These therapy sessions always made him feel better. Dr. Denby was the most amazing psychiatrist in the world. He always said exactly what William wanted to hear.

Elizabeth screamed one last time. It was no use. Yelling hadn't accomplished a thing except making her throat hurt. Even if there had been someone down here to hear her—and there wasn't—the ancient stone walls were too thick for sound to carry through anyway.

Her fingers were beginning to cramp, but she continued to cling to the bookshelf as if it were a life raft. She didn't dare let go. Who knew what could be out there in that impenetrable darkness?

She reached back tentatively with one foot—as far as she could without losing body contact with the books. *Nothing.*

Was there a wall behind her? A room? A tunnel? If she moved off the wooden step, would there be a floor . . . or maybe just an endless deep pit? A drop to nothingness? A fall into an underground river?

Calm down, she told herself. *Be reasonable. You aren't in a dungeon.*

She was suddenly reminded of Tom's CyberDreams. All week he'd been fantasizing about rescuing her from one danger after another. So where was he now that she really needed him?

It was a crazy thought. Tom had no way of

knowing she was in trouble. Besides, after last night Tom was out of the picture—virtual or real. She was on her own. She had to think logically and get herself out of this mess somehow.

As her initial hysteria ebbed, her senses began to kick back in one at a time. And now she smelled something. An awful, putrid, rotting smell. Like something . . . dead. Remembering John Petrie's warnings about bad smells and rats, she was almost relieved—for a moment.

But if it's a rat, she thought, fighting back a wave of nausea, *it's one mondo rat.* The smell was way too bad for one measly rotting rodent to make. *Maybe it's a whole nest of rats.* That thought didn't make her feel any better.

She wrinkled her nose and placed her hand over it. Could she be in some sort of tomb or mausoleum? What if there were racks of dead bodies just a few steps away? Elizabeth suddenly envisioned herself in the catacombs beneath Paris, where ancient skeletons lay stacked like firewood.

I'm being ridiculous! There's nothing like that in the USA—not in California anyway.

An even worse thought suddenly came to mind. What if she was smelling the rotten remains of the last person who'd accidentally grabbed the mysterious yellow book and been whirled into the black void? Was that the fate that awaited her? Would she use up the last of the noxious-smelling air and suffocate? Or would she simply stand in the darkness until she passed out from hunger and exhaustion? Would she lie on the wooden step, clinging to the bookshelf until her rotting corpse added to the hideous smell that already permeated the darkness?

"You're getting morbid here, Wakefield," she muttered to herself. "What are you trying to do? Scare yourself into a heart attack?"

Elizabeth shifted against the bookcase. Whether it was due to her change of position or the fact that her eyes were growing used to the darkness, she could suddenly make out a tiny line of light around the frame of the bookshelf. Elizabeth became encouraged. Although the glowing hairline sliver didn't produce enough light to see by, it at least let her know that she wasn't going to suffocate. If she was sealed up in an airtight tomb, light couldn't seep in, could it?

"OK. I'm not going to suffocate, but . . ." Her words dwindled off. The situation still seemed hopeless.

"Show some initiative," she urged herself. "A little guts. Come on, Elizabeth. You aren't a helpless twit. You've got brains. How are you going to get out of this mess?"

Her little pep talk seemed to revive her mental functions—because suddenly Elizabeth got an idea. If pulling on one book had gotten her in here, pulling on another might get her out.

She felt her way to the right-hand edge of the

shelf and yanked on the first book nearest the wood. It came away easier than she'd expected and flew over her shoulder, landing somewhere behind her with an echoing bang. *Well, at least I know there's a floor back there somewhere,* she consoled herself.

She pulled on the next book in line, being more careful this time. One by one she worked her way down the shelf, tilting each book toward her. When nothing happened, she'd slide it back into place and move to the next one.

When she had tried every single book on the shelf, she began running her fingers along the edges of the shelves themselves. If there was a trip wire for getting her in here, there was bound to be one for getting her out.

Finally, after what seemed like aeons, her fingers touched a little indentation off the side of the bookcase on the stone wall. Inside it seemed to be a latch of some sort.

Elizabeth pulled it.

And with only the slightest squeak the bookshelf swung around again, bringing her back to the cubicle where she'd been working. The bare lightbulb, which had seemed so dim earlier, now seemed like a bright, welcoming beacon.

"Whew!" The place smelled better too.

Elizabeth leaped off the wooden step and away from the bookcase. With hardly a backward glance she shoved her notebook, catalog list, and ink pens into her backpack. She'd uncovered enough historical mysteries for one day. What she needed now was some fresh air and some good ol' California sunshine.

Hearing Elizabeth's key in the lock, Jessica jumped up and ambushed her sister at the door.

"The most awful thing has happened!" she said before bursting into uncontrollable tears.

Elizabeth walked her over to her bed and did her sisterly best to calm her down. But despite all the hugging, patting, and cooing, Jessica wasn't about to be soothed. Her whole world was on the brink of disaster, and she was so overwrought, she was barely able to explain about the lost necklace.

"And Lila was no help at all," she finished with a loud sniff. "Forget that we've been very best friends since elementary school. When I needed her most, she just threw a major prima-donna tantrum and stalked off. She said the only reason I hung around with her was for her money. Can you imagine that?"

"What did you say to her?" Elizabeth asked, passing over a box of tissues.

"Nothing! She wouldn't even lend me the money to pay for the necklace."

"Jessica! I can't believe you would ask Lila for that much money."

Jessica dabbed at her eyes. "Well, she has plenty. She'd never even miss it."

"That's beside the point. You don't ask your friends—"

"Elizabeth, forget her. What're *we* going to do about the missing necklace?" Jessica squawked desperately.

Elizabeth hardly took time to consider the magnitude of the problem. She just fell back on one of her pat answers. "We'll have to tell Mom and Dad."

"Nuh-uh. No way!" Jessica threw up her hands. "Think about what you're saying. They already think I'm irresponsible. If we go running to them, they'll kill me."

"They won't *kill* you, Jessica."

"Well, they'll lock me away for the rest of my life, and *that'll* kill me." Jessica jumped to her feet. "Come on, you're the brainy one. Think of something! You've got to help me. I'm going crazy."

She picked up the empty jewelry case and looked inside it for about the hundredth time since she'd realized the necklace was gone. It was like wiggling a loose tooth. It hurt like crazy, but she just couldn't help doing it. She threw the box down in frustration, then turned back to Elizabeth. "How much money do you have in your account?"

"You've got to be kidding, Jess. That necklace was, like—"

"I know you don't have enough money to buy

it, but I was thinking maybe we could buy a copy or something."

"Don't even think it!"

"Then you'd better come up with a better plan fast. I'm desperate!"

"Why don't I help you look? Where did you last see the necklace?"

"In that defective jewelry case!" Jessica shouted, exasperated that her sister could be so dense.

"Jessica, do you want my help or not? Concentrate. Where were you the last time you opened the case and looked at the necklace?"

"It was when we showed it to William." Jessica gasped. "Oh! You don't think he . . . no . . ." She shook her head, dismissing the thought. "No. I remember looking at the necklace again while we were walking across the quad *after* talking to William. But that was the last time I actually saw the necklace."

"Have you looked here in the room?"

"Of course I have. I turned the place upside down!"

"OK, let's retrace our steps from our room back to the quad."

"It's no use! I've already looked all over the quad and in the lobby downstairs. *And* in the hallway . . . the elevator . . . the stairwell . . . everywhere!"

Elizabeth pursed her lips and gave her a motherly "I know you" look. "Like you looked

191

for your history book the other day . . . when it was right there on your shelf the whole time?"

Jessica paused. Slowly some of the weight that was squeezing against her chest lightened. Maybe Elizabeth was right. Sometimes she *did* manage to overlook things that were hidden in plain sight. With her twin by her side there was still hope. If anyone could help her out of this jam, it was Elizabeth.

Elizabeth shoved another prickly branch out of her face and pushed herself up onto her knees. "There's nothing under here," she called to Jessica.

"I *told* you, I already looked there," Jessica said, offering Elizabeth a hand up.

Elizabeth climbed to her feet. "I know you *said* you looked, but you could have overlooked—"

"I would never overlook diamonds and pearls! And neither would you." Jessica kicked a rock and sent it skittering across the sidewalk. "It's hopeless! We've both covered every inch of this quad and found exactly nothing. Zip. Nada." She dropped heavily onto a nearby concrete bench. "Why is it that every time things start going good for me, something has to happen to ruin it? I think I'm jinxed!"

Elizabeth sank down beside Jessica and wrapped a comforting arm around her back. They sat there quietly like bookless bookends, hugged together in the center of a shelf. Not only did Elizabeth feel sorry for Jessica, but she felt incredibly guilty for letting her down. All her life she'd been the caretaker twin, and now it seemed there was nothing she could do to help. She hated seeing her sister in so much pain.

What can I do? she thought. Her brain had been so scrambled lately, it seemed she couldn't even think straight. *If only Tom were here to—*

"I know," Elizabeth said, leaping from the bench. "Let's stop by WSVU."

"Oh, great," Jessica said bitterly. "I'm having a life crisis here, and you want to go play kissy face with your boyfriend. Thanks a lot, Elizabeth."

"I was thinking that maybe we could convince Tom to broadcast something on tonight's campus news show. Maybe someone already found the necklace on the quad. I'm sure they'd return it if they knew who it belonged to and how important it was."

Jessica straightened her spine and seemed to brighten. "Well . . . I suppose it couldn't hurt. . . ." The corners of her mouth turned up until a dimple appeared in her left cheek. "Maybe good old dull Tom is finally going to be useful for once!" Without waiting for Elizabeth she jumped up and started jogging down the sidewalk.

"Jessica!" Elizabeth called. She was suddenly having second thoughts about the whole idea. Not that she didn't want Tom's help, but after the way he'd acted last night, she wasn't so sure she wanted to ask him for a favor. "Don't get your hopes up," she said, catching up to her sister. "It's possible no one has found the necklace. And not everyone watches the campus news, so it may not do any good."

Jessica shrugged. "Even if no one responds to Tom's broadcast, he can still help us. Don't you get it? If no one finds the necklace, you can ask Tom to lend us the money to pay for it. He's got that huge trust fund now. He might as well use it on something . . . uh, useful."

"I don't think he's *that* rich," Elizabeth said. She was literally dragging her feet, trying to slow Jessica down.

"Sure he is! He can't hold a candle to Bruce or Lila, but he's got more money than he'll ever spend—with his boring lifestyle. And we both know he'd do anything you asked him to do."

"Don't be too sure," Elizabeth muttered under her breath. She kept remembering how blotchy and red his face had turned just before he'd stormed out of her room last night.

But Jessica apparently hadn't heard a word. She was already several yards ahead again.

"You go talk to Tom," she yelled over her shoulder. "I'm going to stop by Theta house and tell Lila the good news." With a happy, exuberant wave she sped up her pace and jogged away, but not before her final words floated back to

Elizabeth—complete with their very own guilt trip.

"You're the best sister in the whole world!"

Elizabeth sighed. Now she had no choice but to go to WSVU and face Tom. She gnawed at the inside of her cheek. It wasn't going to be easy, but she was more than willing to throw herself to the lions. Anything to help Jessica.

Chapter
Eleven

"Really?" Tom tilted back in his chair and made a little tepee with his fingers. He looked up into Elizabeth's big, blue-green eyes. "That's a very sad story, Elizabeth. But I'm pretty busy these days."

"Tom, I'm not asking you to do all that much. I'll even write the copy. All you'll have to do is read it on the air."

He made a clucking noise with his tongue and shook his head. "You know as well as I do, we can't put personal ads on the six o'clock news."

"Not even for me?"

"For you?" He let out a snort somewhere between a laugh and a cough and dropped his hands. "Well, aren't you special?"

The fact that she flinched only drove him onward. He let his chair fall forward with a bang and stood up so that he could tower over her as he let her have it. "You've got a lot of nerve coming in here and asking me to do you a favor. All week you've avoided me like the plague. Every time I've come near you, you've either ignored me or pushed me away. After we fought, you turned up your holier-than-thou little nose at my peace offering, and then, if that weren't enough, you even threw my expensive flowers in the trash."

Elizabeth stared blankly. Her gaze hovered somewhere between Tom's left ear and the enormous calendar he kept on the wall behind his desk.

"For days you've treated me like I'm nothing more than a big, annoying pest," he went on. "And that little tantrum of yours in the mall— well, that was a real showstopper. Do you have any idea how people looked at me after you stood there shrieking that I was a stalker? And now, the minute you need a little favor, you come running to good ol' trusty Tom."

"Tom, I know I've—"

He held up his hand to hush her. "Save the excuses for somebody who cares." He pushed closer, knowing she'd back up. "You know, it's odd that I've never noticed it before, but you're every bit as conniving as Jessica. You both think it's perfectly OK to use your friends to get whatever you want. Well, Miss Wakefield, you've used me for the last time."

Elizabeth was as pale as skim milk and looked

about as weak. "I—I . . . I'm not asking for me, Tom. Couldn't you do it for Jessica?"

"Give me one good reason why I should help you help your ditzy twin."

"*Please,* Tom. Jessica has really gotten herself into deep trouble this time. If we don't recover that necklace, we'll be responsible for it."

"So? Why should I care?"

"Tom! You know Jessica and I can't afford diamonds and pearls from Donantelli's."

"It sounds like Jessica's problem to me. But then, you never *could* let her deal with her troubles on her own. If you're intent on mothering her as usual, then why didn't you start yesterday when she talked you into this crazy scheme? Why did you ever let her come home with a necklace that expensive?"

"Be serious!"

"I am *dead* serious. Jessica is always getting into some idiotic scheme, and you're always bailing her out. How is she ever going to grow up if you don't let her take responsibility once in a while? It's not your job to raise Jessica. And it's sure not *mine.*"

"OK. I understand that you're mad at *me.* But I can't believe you'd take it out on Jessica. She's never done anything to you."

"Don't go there, Elizabeth. That's a can of worms you don't *even* want to get me started on."

Without another word Elizabeth spun around

and stormed out of the office, slamming the door hard enough to rattle the tape cases on the shelf above Tom's head.

"Well, how does that feel, babe?" he muttered. "For once *you* get to be the one who's so mad, you can't do anything except run away."

When he plopped back into his desk chair, she seemed to be staring up at him from her picture on his desk. "It serves you right!" he snarled, flipping the picture over, facedown. "If you don't want to be the princess of my dreams, then don't come in here expecting me to bow and scrape and do your bidding."

He pressed the heels of his hands against his burning eyes. "Why did I do that?" he muttered. "There was no reason for me to act like the world's biggest jerk."

Was there?

He swallowed loudly, but it didn't remove the lump in his throat. He couldn't believe he'd been so harsh and hateful. Why had he deliberately tried to make her mad enough to run away, when all he'd wanted for weeks was to get closer to her? Laying his arms across his desk, he dropped his head onto them and moaned miserably. He couldn't help but feel that he'd just driven the final wedge between himself and the woman he loved.

Elizabeth barely had her key in the lock before Jessica jerked open the door.

"Is it all set up?" Jessica asked impatiently. "We can watch Tom's news broadcast down in the TV lounge if you want."

"I'm sorry, Jess." Elizabeth eased around her sister and dropped tiredly into her desk chair. "I did the best I could, but Tom wouldn't even consider reporting your lost necklace as a news item."

"Well, what about the money? Is he going to give us a loan?"

"No." Elizabeth didn't have the heart to tell her twin that she hadn't even asked. But what would have been the point? The way Tom had been acting, asking for a bigger favor would have only been asking for more humiliation. Why give him the satisfaction?

"No? Just like that?" Jessica's voice wavered pathetically.

"He won't help at all, Jess. He's mad at me, so he's being a bullheaded jerk, basically."

"Well, that doesn't have anything to do with *me*, does it? Can't you just tell him you're sorry for whatever it was, and—"

"No. I can't!" Elizabeth's temper flared. She'd already swallowed her pride by crawling back to him and begging for his help in the first place. And what had it accomplished? Nothing!

Jessica's lower lip trembled, and Elizabeth melted as usual. "C'mon, Jess. You know I would if I could, but it's hopeless. Tom won't budge.

Not as stubborn as he is. Just forget it. Tom's help is not an option."

"Then what are we going to do?" Jessica threw herself dramatically across her bed and burst into tears.

Elizabeth felt like throwing herself down beside her twin and doing the same thing. Not only was she miserable—she was furious. Tom knew very well how much Jessica meant to her. He'd refused to help just to be a heartless, cruel creep. He'd shown his true colors today—whatever color *rotten* was. She could forgive him a lot of things, but not turning his back on Jessica when she desperately needed help. What did Jessica ever do to him anyway?

She moved across the room, leaned down, and patted Jessica's back. "Come on, Jess. Cheer up. I'll make us a cup of tea."

"Tea won't help!" Jessica wiped her cheeks, leaving streaks of mascara.

But in a way it did. Standing there with the tea bags in her hand, Elizabeth remembered doing the same for William. The way he'd treated Jessica in the quad yesterday—he had been so understanding and patient.

Elizabeth dropped the tea bags and grabbed a diet Coke from the minifridge. "You're right. Tea won't help. Here, have one of these instead."

Jessica caught the bottle and raised her tear-streaked face in puzzlement. "Where are you going?"

"Don't give up hope, Jess. I just thought of someone who might help us. I'll be back soon."

Elizabeth made it as far as the front glass doors of Dickenson Hall before the reality of her action stopped her dead in her tracks. The whole campus lay in front of her, and beyond that, all of Sweet Valley. Where did she think she was going? She had no idea where William lived. Even if he was still at Dr. Denby's clinic, which she doubted, she didn't know the name of the clinic. She couldn't even remember Dr. Denby's first name. And people thought Jessica was the one who plowed ahead without planning!

She reached back for the door in resignation. But seeing her pathetic face reflected there reminded her of Jessica's own. She couldn't let her sister down. The least she could do was try.

Think! Always before she'd seen William in the quad or the library. Yes—the library! She'd try there first.

Am I dreaming? William raised his head from the book of Shakespearean sonnets and looked around sleepily.

There it was again. He wasn't dreaming. Someone was actually calling his name.

He closed the book, crooked his head to one side, and turned his good ear toward the sound. *No, not just someone—*

Elizabeth.

William could hardly believe his ears. Her soft, whispery voice floated through the air ducts like heavenly music.

He smiled. Elizabeth was in the library, and she was looking for him.

Within moments William had scurried out of his secret hiding place and into the basement storage closet. Quietly he uncovered the peephole he'd created. It gave him a narrow but clear view of the stacks where he'd chatted with Elizabeth.

There she stood. Upset, but as beautiful as a vision. He watched as she cupped her delicate hands around her mouth like a megaphone and called his name again in a hoarse whisper. His heart was pounding with hopeful excitement as he smoothed his hair and straightened his shirt. His dreams had come true—almost.

Quietly and quickly he slipped through his secret doorway from darkness into the bright, sterile light of the library basement. His soft-soled shoes didn't make a sound on the worn-smooth concrete floor as he hurried up behind her.

When he reached out and tapped her on the shoulder, she jumped.

"Sorry," he said. "I didn't mean to scare you, but I thought I heard you calling my name."

"William! It's you!" She laid a soft white hand against her chest and let out a relieved breath. "I *was* calling you. I hoped I'd find you here. I need your help . . . desperately."

"You know I'd do anything for you, Elizabeth."

"Well, it's not really for *me* . . . I mean, it is, but it isn't. It's Jessica."

"What happened?" he asked anxiously.

"Remember that necklace we showed you yesterday? She lost it. If we don't find it, we're going to have to pay for it. And you saw it. You know how expensive it was! We're both going crazy and . . . and I didn't know where else to turn."

"I'm honored that you would think of me."

"You'll help?"

"I couldn't deny help to your beautiful twin any more than I could deny you. You can count on me to do whatever I can." He rubbed his chin thoughtfully. "OK, we know you had the necklace on the quad when you talked to me. Where did you go after that?"

"Straight to the dorm. Jessica was sure she laid the necklace on her desk, but the next time she opened the box, the necklace wasn't there. The quad is the last place she can remember seeing it."

"I warned Jessica that the clasp was loose. I'll bet it fell out somewhere. Have you tried retracing your steps back to the dorm?"

"We've looked everywhere, William. I think it's hopeless."

"Nothing is ever hopeless. Why don't you and I go out and take another look in the quad. . . ." William's voice dwindled away as he watched tears pool in Elizabeth's eyes. "Let's just give it another try," he continued, taking her by the elbow and leading her toward the stairwell. "And if we don't find it, I can always lend you the money to cover it with the jeweler."

"Really?" she asked, her voice frail. "You would do that for us?"

William covered her hand with his. "What are friends for?"

"Oh, William . . . thank you. Thank you so much."

Then, miracle of miracles, Elizabeth grabbed him and hugged him.

Jessica slumped on the concrete bench. Her arms, which were hugged tightly around her knees, provided no comfort. Even though the day was warm and sunny, she felt only cold—from the sensation of the cool concrete against the seat of her jeans to the icy dread that gripped her heart. She shivered. She had never been so miserable in her whole life.

This is all just a waste of time, she thought as she watched her sister and William White crawl around on their hands and knees on the grassy quad.

"Jessica, aren't you going to help?" Elizabeth asked.

"Why bother?" She sighed. "We've already covered every square inch of this quad—twice."

"You shouldn't give up so easily." William sat back on his heels and ran a hand through his gorgeous blond hair. She was glad she couldn't see his whole face from where she sat—just his handsome side. "C'mon, Jessica. Keep the faith. Especially now that you've got me on the case."

"What makes you think *you* can find the necklace after Elizabeth and I failed?"

"I don't know. I've got sort of a sixth sense when it comes to finding lost things."

"Oh, really? What lost things have you found lately?" Although Jessica's tone was cynical, deep down she actually wanted his reassurance.

"Well, I've found lots of things lately. Haven't I, Elizabeth? . . . Like my honor, my soul, and my own sense of morality, for example."

Jessica didn't understand what he was talking about or the goofy look he gave Elizabeth, and she really didn't care about interpreting their personal jokes. She saw nothing funny in the entire situation.

"Jess." Elizabeth dusted off her jeans and walked over to where she sat. "I know you're upset, but don't take it out on William. I think it was very sweet of him to come out here and help us look." She leaned closer and whispered in her ear, "And William has agreed to lend us the money if we don't find the necklace. So cheer up."

"You're right. I'm sorry." Jessica's voice quivered as she fought to keep from crying. "But even if he lends us the money we need, what good is it? We'll be a hundred and ten before we can ever get him paid back!"

Elizabeth's shoulders sagged. "Maybe so, but so far, he's the only friend who has offered to help."

Jessica watched her sister jog back to William's side. He pointed to something in the grass and the two of them took off in that direction.

"It's nothing but a candy wrapper," Jessica mumbled. She could see it from where she sat. But Elizabeth was right about one thing. It was sweet of William to try. He was a guy with manners and good breeding. Elizabeth could do worse . . . in fact, she had. Tom Watts was an idiot for treating Elizabeth like a piece of property and a monster for abandoning them in their time of need. Some boyfriend he'd turned out to be.

"We're going to try over here, Jess," Elizabeth called over her shoulder as she and William started toward some bushes.

Jessica groaned. Why crawl around again under the same exact bushes that she'd already crawled around until her back ached? It was hopeless, hopeless, hopeless.

"Let's just forget about it," Jessica grumbled, getting to her feet. "I'll just drop out of school, declare bankruptcy, get a menial job, and forget the whole rest of my life. I didn't want to be happy again anyway."

"Eureka!" William yelled from behind a flowering shrub. Although he was out of her sight, Jessica's heart began to pound excitedly. Dare she get her hopes up? Did William mean what she thought he meant?

"I found it!" he exclaimed. As he climbed out from under the shrub's drooping branches, Jessica stared at the hand he held above his head. Something dangled from his fingers—something sparkling.

Whooping for joy, she ran at him so fast, she almost couldn't stop. She snagged the necklace from his hand as she skidded past and held it against her heart.

"William White! I could kiss you!" she cried ecstatically. "You're absolutely the best. You have my permission to hang around with my sister for as long as she lives!"

As Elizabeth watched her sister dance around with the necklace clutched to her heart, tears blurred her vision. She felt as if she'd just slipped from a hangman's knot. She hadn't let on to Jessica just how worried she'd really been about the lost necklace. Although she knew her parents would have helped them out, it would have been a terrible hardship on the whole family. But now everything was all right again—thanks, unbeliev-ably enough, to William White.

"Are you OK?" William whispered nearby.

"Yes . . . oh, I'm just so relieved!" She wiped away a tear with her knuckle and smiled her grati-tude. How incredible that William would come through for her like that! When she came right down to it, it was odd that she'd turned to him for help in the first place. But it was almost as if she knew he would succeed where everyone else had failed her.

And he had. He'd seemed to pluck that neck-lace out of thin air. She could clearly remember looking all around that bush earlier in the after-noon and finding nothing. But it only proved how terribly upset she had been. She'd been so worried and frightened for Jessica's sake that she hadn't been seeing straight.

"Jessica, take that necklace straight back to our room!" she ordered, turning around to her sister. Jessica didn't even gripe about being bossed around or mothered. She was evidently too full of gratitude as well.

"Don't worry. I've learned my lesson. I'm tak-ing this thing straight to the dorm office and hav-ing them lock it in their safe until tomorrow night."

"Thank you, William," Elizabeth said as Jessica bounced across the quad toward Dickenson Hall. "I know we've put you to a lot of trouble. I owe you—really, really owe you, big time. If there's ever anything I can do for you, just let me know."

William kicked at a clump of grass. "Actually . . . there is something you could do."

"Anything. You just name it."

"Well . . ." He stared at his shoes a moment. "How about a date tomorrow night?"

"I'm serious, William. Don't tease me. You have literally saved Jessica's future, and I don't know how we can ever repay you."

"I am completely serious," William countered. "I can't think of anything I'd rather have in this world than your company."

Elizabeth paused. Should she accept? She couldn't help but remember how close they'd come to kissing in her room last night. Was that what she wanted?

Yes? No?

She was torn between desire and fear . . . between caution and a true, aching need to do something out of the ordinary.

William moved over so that only his left side was facing her. She wanted to tell him he didn't have to do that. But as she gazed at his startlingly handsome face, she lost her train of thought. His left eye, so brilliantly blue, looked at her with a sweetness that was almost breathtaking. There was no madness, no meanness, no insanity shining there. No hate tensed his jaw muscles. He seemed completely relaxed and peaceful—inside as well as

211

out. Even knowing his past, she could only see concern and caring in his expression.

"Please, Elizabeth. Just one date. That's not too much to ask, is it? I mean, if you have a free night. I know how busy you are. But—no pressure."

A free night? After the way Tom had acted at WSVU this afternoon, she had nothing but free nights ahead of her. For a long moment she compared the twisted anger of Tom's face to the calm, peaceful look on William's. "OK. Friday sounds fine to me."

William paced around the dimly lit room until Dr. Denby ordered him to sit.

"Sorry." He calmly sat down on the couch, but his hands flew up like agitated birds. "I'm just so excited."

"I take it your plan worked."

"The most wonderful thing has finally happened, Dr. Denby. Elizabeth has agreed to go out with me again."

"I can see that you are very happy, William."

"Happy doesn't begin to describe what I'm feeling. I'm ecstatic." William rocked back and forth on the couch eagerly. He was so elated, he couldn't contain his energy. "I've waited so long for her, and now finally she's going to be mine. Elizabeth and I are going to be together forever."

"Don't get overly optimistic, William. Things could still—"

"No. Don't even say it." William slapped his hands over his ears. "Elizabeth and I are going to be together, and I'm not going to let anything spoil it this time."

"You did last time. You scared her away."

"Not this time. I'm being very careful, and I won't do anything foolish. You'll see. I can't take a chance on losing her again."

William walked over to Dr. Denby, knelt on the floor in front of him, and stared into his somber face. "I need her, Dr. Denby. I need Elizabeth even as much as I need you. The two of you are the only people in the world I trust. I couldn't stand it if I lost either of you . . . not ever!"

"I'm here for you, William."

"I know. Forever." He patted the good doctor's outstretched hand. "And soon Elizabeth will be too."

Chapter Twelve

Stunning. Absolutely divine, Jessica thought, running her hands down the side of her slinky purple dress. *I look fabulous. Charles is going to die when he sees me!* She looked over at her sister and exhaled loudly. "Elizabeth, are you going to hog the mirror all night?"

Why was it that a dorm room seemed to shrink to postage-stamp size when two women tried to get ready for dates at the same time?

"Scoot over," Jessica demanded. "I need to check my hair." She elbowed her way between Elizabeth and the mirror.

"You've checked it five times already. It still looks fine."

"Fine isn't good enough. It's got to look perfect!"

"Oh, silly me! Did I say fine? I meant absolutely spectacular."

"Be real, OK?" Jessica craned her neck to view herself from the side. "I put it up like this so my necklace would show more, but I don't know if an up do is really me. Do you think I should wear it down?"

"No. I like it up. And while we're on the subject of hair," Elizabeth said as she twisted her last pale strand of hair into a neat-looking French braid, "how's this?"

"It beats your usual boring ponytail," Jessica said offhandedly as she took her new royal purple heels from their box.

"I thought we'd decided you liked my ponytail."

"Hmmm?" Jessica murmured absently as she stepped into her shoes.

"The other day, before we went to the mall . . . oh, never mind."

Jessica hurried over to the full-length mirror. "Don't you think these shoes match my dress perfectly?"

"Does it really matter what I think?" Elizabeth mumbled.

Jessica raised an eyebrow at her sister but decided not to pursue it. She was so excited, she could hardly stand it. She didn't want anything to spoil her mood before the IM Awards gala.

Elizabeth turned her back and stepped into a casual, sleeveless, white sheath dress with floral accents. "Zip me, please."

216

"Where are you and William going anyway?" Jessica asked, zipping the dress.

"I don't know for sure. He just said dinner at one of his favorite places."

"I'll bet it's going to be fancy and you're going to be way underdressed," Jessica said, pursing her lips. "Don't you think you should wear something a little more, uh . . . elegant? Want to borrow something of mine?"

"No, this will be fine. If William had wanted me to dress up, he'd have said so."

Jessica watched her sister fidget with her hem. "What's wrong, Liz?"

"I don't know. Is something *supposed* to be wrong?"

"No! You just seem—well, like you're nervous or something. Like your heart's not really in it."

Elizabeth shrugged.

Jessica always knew that when Elizabeth stopped talking, she was bugged about something. "If you don't want to go on this date, don't."

"I want to go . . . I think. I'm just sort of worried, I guess."

"Well, if you're worried that William is a monster or something, I think you can relax. He's only scary on the outside. Just stay on his left side and you'll be fine. He seems nice enough to me." Jessica caressed the pearls at her neck. "I think he's just a big old marshmallow."

"William's scars don't scare me, Jess. And neither

does the past . . . not anymore. I really do believe that he's changed. I don't think there's a drop of evil left in him. But William isn't really the problem. It's me. I'm totally confused right now about what I'm feeling. I'm attracted to William, but a lot of my anxiety is over Tom."

"You think he's going to stalk you and find you with William and scream bloody murder? You know, it's like a totally perfect revenge scenario."

"No. Jeez, I hope not. Anyway, it's nothing like that. I just wonder if maybe I should have told Tom about William."

"Oooh, bad idea! You know how jealous he is. Besides, it's none of his business. You two broke up again, right?"

"I think so. Yeah, I guess we did. Actually, that's the problem. My brain knows we broke up, but in my heart I don't really feel like we did. I sort of feel like I'm cheating on Tom."

"Don't think about him! You don't owe him a thing, not after the way he bailed on us yesterday."

The phone rang, and Jessica began to jump around excitedly. "That's my limo!" She dashed toward the phone and snagged it before Elizabeth had a chance. "Hellooo," Jessica said in a low, Marilyn Monroe whisper.

"Jess? Is that you? It's me, Tom."

Jessica not only dropped the sexy voice, but also any pretense of being friendly. "Oh, hello, *Tom*." She said the name loudly for Elizabeth's benefit and pantomimed gagging herself with a finger down her throat. "What can we do for you tonight? Oh, *that's* right! We're not doing favors for each other anymore, are we?"

"Uh . . . I was just wondering if you found your necklace," he said in a totally insincere, fake-polite way.

Jessica rolled her eyes. "Yes. We found it. But no thanks to you, you creep!"

Click.

Jessica blinked in surprise. Tom actually had the nerve to hang up on her! She stared at the buzzing receiver for a moment and then slammed it back onto its cradle. "Well, that's the end of that," she said to her twin. "He didn't even ask about you. Now you can quit feeling guilty about poor, mistreated Tom and go out and have a good time for once!"

Elizabeth nodded, but she didn't look any more convinced. "Which shoes?" she asked quietly. "Sandals or slip-ons?"

"Slip-ons," Jessica advised. "And here. Wear my new sweater." Jessica didn't usually like lending her clothes—especially new ones. But Elizabeth was definitely in need of some cheering up. Besides, Elizabeth didn't know it yet, but her credit card had paid for it.

Elizabeth took the sweater and held it up against her dress. "Yes, Mom, but it's not that cold out."

"I know. But layering is all-important. If you don't know where you're going, then you need to be prepared for anything. Come on, you can just tie it around your shoulders. It'll bring out the green in those flowers, and if you do happen to get chilly, you've got it."

Elizabeth draped the sweater over her shoulders and looped the sleeves in front of her neck. "Do I look all right?"

"Not as good as me, but you'll do," Jessica teased.

Elizabeth reached for the door.

"Hey, Liz! Smile. Have fun. And don't worry about missing me on television. They're taping the whole show over at Theta house. We can watch it tomorrow."

Elizabeth pasted on a grin and softly closed the door behind her.

What a shame, Jessica thought. Her sister was acting more as if she were walking to her own firing squad than on her way to a fun Friday-night date. Well, that's what happened when someone stuck with the same guy too long. After an eternity with a big old bore like Tom Watts, anyone would forget that the whole dating process was supposed to be an adventure. A total adventure!

Stopping in front of the mirror, she checked her hair once more. Elizabeth was right. The up do was absolutely spectacular. She turned on a full-force smile, dimple and all. "Look out, Hollywood. Jessica Wakefield is baa-aack!"

For once Elizabeth was glad she had taken Jessica's advice. The slip-ons were definitely the right choice. With as much walking as she and William had done the past hour, sandals would have been a disaster. She would have had blisters galore.

"Are you getting tired?" William asked, his voice deep with concern.

"No. It's so beautiful and peaceful out tonight. I'm enjoying the walk."

"You aren't disappointed, are you?" he asked for the third time as they neared the quad again. "I know you're used to more exciting dates."

If you only knew how boring my life has been lately, she replied silently. She smiled at him and tried to reassure him. "Don't give it another thought. I'm having a wonderful time."

"I know you deserve better. It's just that I'm not ready to face the world. If we went to a restaurant or a movie, I know people would stare. And that wouldn't be much fun for either of us. I'd just die if I thought you were ashamed to be seen with me."

"I'm not ashamed." She turned to face him, but her tender moment was spoiled when her stomach growled loudly. She cringed with embarrassment and prayed he hadn't heard. But seeing his grin, she knew he had.

"Excuse me," Elizabeth said, feeling the blood rush to her face. "I was so busy today, I didn't take time for lunch. All I've had since breakfast is a few crackers."

"And your date promised you dinner."

"That's OK. I'm fine, really."

"Don't be silly. I'd say it's time we feed you."

"But you said . . . I don't want to go anywhere you're uncomfortable."

"Well, tonight we're eating at a place where I'm totally comfortable. I think you will be too."

"Where are we going?"

"To the library."

"The library?" Elizabeth choked back a laugh. "We can't take food in the library!" Immediately she wanted to smack herself on the forehead. Jeez, she sounded just like John Petrie.

He smiled mysteriously. "It's already there waiting for us. We're having a catered picnic in the geography lab."

"Are you serious?" Elizabeth glanced at the clock tower at the far end of the quad. "But the library closes early on Friday nights. It'll only be open a few more minutes."

"I know. That's why we've been walking all over creation—killing time."

None of this was making sense to her. "If it's closed, how are we going to get in?"

"There are ways. You know how you sneaked me into your dorm through the fire stairs? Well, I know how to get into the library anytime I want."

"You're kidding! How?"

"Come with me and you'll see." Taking her hand, William led her around the sidewalk to the back of the library. Slipping between some bushes, they stepped down three crumbling concrete steps to a rickety wooden door. He opened it easily and held it for her. Four more concrete steps led to the basement level.

"This used to be a service entrance back when the boilers had to be tended at night," he explained as he closed the door behind them. "I doubt anyone even remembers it's back here. It's been blocked off for years."

Elizabeth's conscience nagged at her. She knew she shouldn't be sneaking into the library after hours. But she squelched it. For the first time in ages she was doing something daring and exciting. She was thoroughly enjoying the wicked, naughty feeling of sneaking in a secret entrance and prowling through her favorite building when no one else on campus knew about it.

They crept through the dark, dusty old boiler room, which had apparently been converted into a storage area. Crooked stacks of discarded books and cardboard boxes loomed in the shadows.

At last they entered a back hallway that was lit by security lights. Locked, labeled doors led off both sides: the media lab, the video storage room, the audio lab. William stopped in front of the door to the geography lab and took out a key.

"You have a key?" Elizabeth clamped a hand over her mouth as her voice echoed around the deserted library.

"It's OK. You can talk normally. No one ever comes down here after hours. Once the security guards have made their initial check, they rarely bother to come back to the basement level all night."

When William pushed open the door, Elizabeth's jaw dropped with surprise. The boring, run-of-the-mill geography lab had been transformed into a virtual flower garden.

Wildflowers were everywhere. Baskets full, boxes full, jars, mugs, and glasses full. There were flowers on map cases, flowers on desks, flowers on projectors and even on the floor. There were flowers on every available surface except for the very center of the floor, where a delicate lace tablecloth had been spread. It had already been set with plates, glasses, silverware, and a flickering candle in a glass holder. A picnic basket, ice bucket, and chilling bottle of wine sat nearby.

"I don't believe this!" she exclaimed. "You went to all this trouble for me?"

"Nothing is too much trouble for you." William knelt beside the picnic basket and began laying out the food. "Come on, Elizabeth. I know you're hungry." He grinned mischievously.

She settled beside him and popped a bacon-wrapped scallop into her mouth. "Delicious," she said. "What's that, spinach dip?"

William opened a tray of fresh, crisp vegetables and then helped himself to a piece of celery. "There are sandwiches and cheese and two kinds of dessert."

For several moments she was too busy tasting all the tempting finger foods to talk. William poured them each a glass of wine.

"This is wonderful, William," she said, wiping her mouth on a linen napkin before taking the delicate stemware from his fingers. "I've never had a picnic like this!" Imagine, a secret picnic in a library after hours. William clearly knew her well.

She set her wineglass on the floor and picked up a book that was lying beside the picnic basket. *Sonnets of Shakespeare.* A sudden cold chill skittered up her spine as she recalled all the sonnets William had bombarded her with when he had stalked her before. "What is this doing here?"

"I was reading it earlier tonight while I was waiting to meet you." He took the book from her hands. He seemed so casual about it. Elizabeth forced herself to relax. "I found one I especially liked. I think you'd enjoy it. Can I read parts of it to you?"

"I guess, if you want to." She helped herself to another sandwich and settled back against the leg of a table while William opened the book to the page he wanted.

> "When, in disgrace . . . I all alone beweep
> my outcast state . . . ,
> And look upon myself, and curse my fate. .
> . ."

The sandwich suddenly tasted like cardboard. William was clearly talking about his own scarred face. Guilty tears welled in Elizabeth's eyes. It was all her fault that he felt like a cursed outcast.

> "Haply I think on thee—and then my state . . .
> . . . sings hymns at heaven's gate;
> For thy sweet love remember'd such
> wealth brings
> That then I scorn to change my state with
> kings."

Elizabeth blushed. Was William saying that he would rather be scarred and hidden away with her than handsome, rich, and alone?

Embarrassed, she fanned her hot face with an empty paper plate. Talk about jumping to conclusions! William had read a simple, yet beautiful, sonnet and she had presumptuously assumed he was talking about her. Thankfully, he couldn't read her mind *that* well.

"What do you think?" he asked, closing the book.

"It was beautiful," she said. She set down her sandwich and wiped her mouth. "It ended hopefully, even though it started out just terribly depressing."

"I know. I love happy endings." He picked up his wineglass and took a sip. "Do you think I'll ever have one, Elizabeth? A happy ending, I mean?"

"I know you will. I'm so glad you found Dr. Denby and got help. It's wonderful the way you were able to put your life back together. I'm . . . I'm proud of you."

He drained his glass and set it aside. "You call sneaking pretty girls into locked libraries getting my life back together?" he asked jokingly.

Realizing she must have embarrassed him with her compliment, she matched his lighter tone. "I know a lot of guys on campus who would say yes to that question."

"I imagine they would," he said with a laugh.

"I hope no one seals that door back up and ruins your dating chances forever," she teased.

He shrugged. "It wouldn't matter. I know lots of other secret ways into the library."

"You're kidding!"

"No. I know more about this library than anyone. My family donated the library to the school, you know. We used to own all this land around here. In fact, my great-great-grandfather's château sat on the very spot where the library is now. He

227

had a huge wine cellar and lots of secret passages that still exist. You've seen a few of them yourself."

"You mean the archives, where I've been working all week?"

He nodded. "What you've seen is only a fraction of the many passages under the library."

"How do you know?"

"My great-grandfather donated the property to the university with the understanding that my grandfather would be the school's chief architect. He actually drew up the plans for the library and several other buildings here on campus."

"The White Memorial Hall?"

"That's one of them. Well, after Granddad killed himself, my mother cleaned out his office almost immediately and threw away nearly everything. But when I saw her tossing out a box of blueprints, I latched onto them for some reason."

"Because they reminded you of your grandfather?"

"Maybe. But more likely, they reminded me of why my grandfather always ignored me. See, when I was little, my mom and I never got along, and I never really knew my dad all that well. I'd try to hang out with my grandfather, but whenever I'd sneak into his office, he'd roar for me to go away, that he was too busy. I'm sure it wasn't even the library blueprints by that time, but I can remember seeing all this blue paper spread on Granddad's drafting table. I guess it's what I associated with him."

Tears came to Elizabeth's eyes. She grabbed her napkin and wiped them away while pretending to wipe her mouth.

"Anyway, I own the only complete set of the original library plans, and I've had them since I was a kid. I've actually been sneaking in here for years."

Elizabeth brushed crumbs from her lap and stood up. "This is rather embarrassing."

"Why?" William scrambled to his feet beside her.

"Because now I know that when I was rattling on and on about the archives when you were in my room Wednesday night, you already knew all about them. You were only listening to be polite."

"Not so." William tilted his head to meet her eyes. "Believe me, I was truly interested in every word you said. It absolutely delighted me to think that you might be as interested in the labyrinth as I am. I hardly dared to dream that you—I mean, any woman—would enjoy exploring dank, dark corridors and digging up history and dusty old volumes of poetry."

"I love it. I've had so much fun working on the archives project. I don't know how to describe it, but it's just . . . thrilling! You just never know what you'll discover down there. Sometimes when I'm working, I wish I could just put my pencil down and go explore."

"You can if you'd really like to. I can show you places the archives committee will never find."

"Really? Now?"

He stood and held out his hand. "If you want to."

"I'd love to!" She let him pull her to her feet. "What about all this?" she asked, pointing to what was left of their picnic.

"It'll be fine here. And don't worry. We'll be fine too. No one knows about my secret places."

She and William slipped quietly from the geography lab, down the hall, and past the basement stacks.

"This way," William said, opening a door that led to a janitor's utility closet.

She looked at him skeptically. But it was a little late to start worrying now. If she felt confident enough to sneak into a deserted library alone with William, then why should she balk at going into a silly closet? If he had evil on his mind, he'd already had plenty of chances to try something.

Elizabeth followed William into the closet, where he pulled some boxes away from the wall. He stooped and removed a small piece of baseboard, which revealed a hidden lever.

"Would you care to do the honor?" he asked.

Elizabeth leaned down and gave the lever a yank. Like magic, a small, waist-high trapdoor opened beneath a shelf.

William ducked inside and reached an arm back out for her. Without a word she took his hand.

She wasn't sure if it was the excitement of entering unexplored territory or William's touch, but she suddenly felt tingles all through her body.

Chapter
Thirteen

"You big, stupid, hotheaded moron," Tom criticized himself as he paced back and forth across his cramped WSVU office. He had been fuming and fretting ever since he'd called Elizabeth's room and got read the riot act by Jessica. "Why in the world didn't I just offer to help Elizabeth when she asked? Would it have been so hard to mention a stupid lost necklace on the news? What's wrong with me?"

He let out a derisive snort. "Pride, that's what," he answered himself. "Lame, obnoxious male pride."

Tom lay back on the beat-up couch he kept in his office and closed his eyes. He felt as if his whole world were falling apart. Elizabeth was the most important thing in the world to him, and he'd driven her away.

"Tom, are you asleep?"

Tom opened one eye and saw Julie Fiore standing in the doorway of his office.

"Yes," he grumbled. "I'm sound asleep."

He thought she'd take the hint and leave, but she bounded cheerily into the room, as if his snarly reply had been an engraved invitation.

"Surely that old couch isn't as comfortable as your dorm bed," she said.

"No, but I'm working."

"On a Friday night? I thought the new girl—namely me—was the only one who got stuck with the Friday-night shift. This schedule can be murder on somebody's love life."

"Assuming somebody had a love life, I guess it would." Tom gave up the pretense of sleeping and sat up.

Julie's habitual grin faded. "Whoa, you look like warmed-over heartbreak. I take it the flowers didn't work."

"She hated them. How was I supposed to know I was in love with the only girl on campus who hates fancy flowers?"

"Maybe that's the problem. Not the flowers," Julie clarified, "but the fact that you didn't know what she liked."

"How was I supposed to know? She never said she hated flowers, and I'm no mind reader."

"She probably doesn't see it as mind reading. Maybe she thinks that if you really loved her, you'd just know her intuitively. Women do it all the time. You know, you just pick up on innocent little comments she makes and read her body language."

"It sounds like a lot of trouble to me."

"If you really love her, it isn't."

He sighed. "I do really love her, Julie. And I know it's not that much trouble—not really. I'm just annoyed because I know you're right. But it's a moot point anyway. Our whole relationship is a wreck."

"Even wrecks are sometimes salvageable."

Tom wanted to believe Julie was right. Was there still hope for him and Elizabeth to work things out? He wanted to believe it with every bone in his body. But he wasn't sure he could.

"Well, why don't you call her?"

"I did," he said, letting his chin slump to his chest.

"What did she say?"

"I . . . well, when her sister answered the phone and called me a creep, I hung up."

"Tom, hanging up on your girlfriend's sister doesn't count. If you want your lady back, then you've got to communicate. Why don't you try calling her again?" Julie leaned over and poked him with a finger. "Go on. Do it right now. I'm already on the schedule, and I think I can take care of the Friday-night rush around here." She grabbed the phone off his desk and with a yank of the cord stretched it to where he sat. "Call."

"It's private," he said, looking sheepishly at her.

"OK. I'm gone." Julie let her smile return to her freckled face and waved good-bye.

The minute she left his office, Tom picked up the phone and dialed Elizabeth's room. As it rang and rang, he began to imagine all the places she could be. She could be at her friend Nina's . . . or at the Red Lion with friends.

He switched the receiver to his other ear and let it ring some more. More than likely, she was out somewhere bailing Jessica out of another mess. Impatient, he hung up. But hardly three heartbeats later he snatched the phone right back up and jabbed redial. Maybe she'd just stepped out of the room for a second.

By the time he'd counted ten more rings, Tom's patience had totally evaporated. "I'll bet she's out with that . . . that *guy!*"

He slammed the receiver down, jumped to his feet, and resumed his earlier pacing and muttering. "Stop it!" he told himself. "It's time to stop being so suspicious. Come on, man. Control this jealousy!"

He picked up Elizabeth's overturned picture and stared at her beautiful, heart-shaped face. He knew Elizabeth. She was probably taking out her frustrations and anger the same way he was—with work. For Tom that meant WSVU. For Elizabeth that could only mean one place—the library.

Tom glanced at his watch and frowned. The library was closed.

Suddenly Tom remembered the very thing Elizabeth had been trying to talk about all week when he hadn't been listening—the newly discovered archives under the library. The committee was probably working after hours to avoid the snooping students and conflicting schedules. Elizabeth was probably there at this very moment, crawling around in some dusty tunnel with a couple of dweebs. And to think he'd just sat there and mentally accused her of chasing after some other *man*. Had he completely lost his mind?

Elizabeth glanced overhead at the string of twinkly little Christmas-tree lights. They weren't very bright, but the glow was enough to see William's shadowy form in front of her as he led her through the labyrinth of corridors beneath the library.

She was amazed at how many twists and turns they'd taken. William had been telling the truth when he'd said she only knew about part of the archives. This place was endless. And she was the only one who knew! Except for William, of course.

"Where does all this come out?" she whispered when they made yet another turn. She felt hopelessly lost, yet excited in a way she couldn't describe.

"Where I live."

Elizabeth blinked. "You live down here?"

"Yes . . . it's not so bad. It's private, and no one else in the world knows about it except Dr. Denby. And now you."

How sad, Elizabeth thought. *Poor William, living down here like a mole, never seeing the light.* It didn't seem fair. "How long have you been living down here?"

"Awhile." He pushed open a heavy oak door. "Here it is. My home sweet home."

They stepped into a small cubicle—one not much bigger than the one she'd been working in all week. William left the door open, but the feeble glow of the Christmas lights didn't penetrate the dark, shadowy room. Two large, scented candles flickered in jars on a library table against one wall.

By their dim light she could make out a dingy old couch right in the center of the room. Farther back in the shadows were a small bookshelf and an ancient file cabinet, almost identical to the one she'd been taking files from all week. Stacks of old books were everywhere.

Elizabeth felt as if she'd been transported to another century. The only indication that the modern world had infiltrated the depths of William's lair was a bright yellow ice chest beside the couch, where an end table would have logically sat. On top of the ice chest lay a perfectly solved Rubik's Cube and a cheap plastic cigarette lighter.

"Have a seat and make yourself at home," William said grandly.

Seeing no other place to sit, Elizabeth perched awkwardly on the edge of the wobbly couch. Judging from the pillows and neatly folded blanket, she could tell this was where he'd been sleeping.

"Why do you live down here?" she asked more bluntly than she'd intended to.

"I told you. I'm not ready to face the outside world."

"Your psychiatrist knows about this, and he says it's OK?"

"Relax, Elizabeth. It's really not as bad as your first impression might lead you to believe. Yes. Dr. Denby knows. He insists I'm cured. There's no reason to keep a perfectly sane person locked away in an asylum, but I haven't been able to make the transition to living in public yet. He and I both decided this was a perfect solution. I think of it as a sort of halfway house where I can get used to living with . . . my appearance."

It was kind of creepy to Elizabeth, but she could see where it might be cozy and comforting to William. At least it was clean. Even in the semi-darkness she could see that William's room contrasted sharply with the dusty passages they'd just come through.

Still, she couldn't shake her slightly queasy feeling. Instead of brightening the dark and dismal

239

room, the candles only served to cast spooky, quivering shadows on the walls. And there was an uneasy smell about the whole place. At first the scented candles had been all she'd noticed, but now that she was farther away from the candles . . . there was something familiar. . . .

Suddenly she remembered being trapped behind the revolving bookshelf. It was the same awful smell. Surely that hideous odor didn't permeate the whole labyrinth.

Elizabeth turned up her nose. But she couldn't escape it. The whole room smelled like death.

"Maybe I should have brought some of the wildflowers down here to cheer the place up a bit," William said, noticing how Elizabeth had wrinkled her nose.

She squinted up at him.

"Poor Elizabeth. You can't see, can you?" He hurried over to the couch. "I apologize. I should have been more insightful about your needs. You're not used to the darkness the way I am." He picked up the plastic lighter from the ice chest and went to work, lighting the row of candles he'd lined atop the bookshelf.

"I bought a whole sackful the other day—well, you know. You saw them," he babbled nervously. He lit a couple more on top of the file cabinet and finally a big one, which he placed on the ice chest next to Elizabeth. He slipped the lighter into his pocket and left his hand there a moment. He didn't want Elizabeth to notice how his hand was shaking.

"Gardenia," he explained. "It'll help take away the dank, musty smell too. It gets sort of damp and mildewy down here sometimes."

She picked up a book that he'd left on the arm of the couch and began leafing through it. "How can you read down here with just the candlelight? Doesn't it give you a headache?"

"Oh, I have electricity, but tonight I thought we'd stick with candles. The place can be a little too depressing in the light. Anyway, the candles are a lot more . . . atmospheric."

She closed the book and smiled crookedly at him.

"Really, Elizabeth. I can tell you're uneasy, but it's not all that bad. I don't have rent or utilities or crabby neighbors to put up with. I come and go as I please, and it's private. I like that best."

William knew he was rambling, but he couldn't help himself. He was too nervous and excited at having Elizabeth sitting here in his home at last.

What if he was moving too quickly? What if he'd rushed her and blown his chances? Hadn't he promised Dr. Denby that nothing would go wrong? "We can go back upstairs if you want," he said timidly. "I don't want you to feel I've—"

"No, it's all right. I'm getting used to it now. You were right about the candles. They're very . . .

uh . . . relaxing, and they smell good too. Come and sit down, William. You're pacing all over the place."

William sat beside her gratefully. His thigh brushed hers on the narrow couch, and his whole body tensed at the nearness of her. As Elizabeth leaned across him to replace the book on the arm of the couch, he could smell the fresh, tangy scent of the shampoo she'd used.

He closed his eyes. It was all he could do to keep from reaching out and caressing that glorious golden hair. But he didn't want to rush her and take a chance on scaring her away.

I wish she'd worn her hair down, he thought. He could just imagine running his fingers through her loose blond hair. *I wish . . .*

Suddenly the hairs on the back of his neck prickled, and he realized she was touching his hand.

"Thanks for the picnic, William. And thanks for showing me your secret hideaway."

Hideaway. He liked that term. It made his rat hole sound romantic, special. He looked at his hand. Her touch was searing through his skin. Slowly he turned toward her. But it was too much. He panicked.

"Wait," he whispered. "Change sides of the couch with me." He jumped to his feet and stepped around her.

She stared at him in confusion as he settled on

the other side of her. Without a word of explanation he situated himself so his right side was in the shadows.

"Don't," she whispered. "You don't have to hide from me, William."

When she laid her gentle white hand against his scarred cheek, William thought his heart would burst. He could stand the wait no more.

Slowly he leaned toward her and touched his lips to hers. It was hardly more than a peck, a gentle, brief touch of his lips to hers, but William felt as if his soul were on fire.

He was totally unprepared for the feelings that exploded inside him when Elizabeth responded. She not only relaxed into his arms, but seemed to melt against him. His kiss became more passionate. When he felt her arm snake around his neck and pull him closer, his heart stopped. His breathing stopped. His world stopped.

He broke away for a moment, just to make sure it was really happening. Her eyes were shut, her cheeks rosy in the candlelight. She was really with him at last. He and Elizabeth would be together always and forever. He was sure of that now.

Closing his eyes again, he leaned in for another kiss.

Suddenly nervous and upset, Elizabeth pushed William away.

"What's wrong?" he whispered. "That kiss . . . it was . . . magical."

That was just the trouble. It had been too magical. She shouldn't have been kissing anyone, let alone William White. And she shouldn't have been liking it. Where was her loyalty to Tom? Where was their relationship?

Where am I?

"Please, William," she said quietly. "I don't know if we should . . ." She scooted away slightly and straightened her skirt. "Let me catch my breath."

William's hand around her wrist tightened— almost as if he'd had a spasm in his fingers. His expression hardened, making her nervous.

She eased farther away from him and rubbed her nose with her free hand. Not only did she feel overwhelmed by her feelings, but the whole creepy room was starting to get to her. The dim light, the dank feel, and the smell . . . that ever present, evil, ugly smell that lingered and mixed with the cloying scent of the candles.

"Try to understand, William," she began carefully. "I like you. I really do, but this is happening so fast." She pulled her wrist free from his grip. Evidently he had no idea how hard he was squeezing her. "Could we just slow down a bit? You know, just get to know each other better?"

William looked as if he'd been slapped.

"Don't be hurt. I'm not rejecting you. I really

do like you, and I've had a wonderful time tonight. But I'm kind of uneasy about it. Would it be cool with you if we sort of take this really . . . slow?"

William leaped from the couch, his hands clenched at his sides. He was suddenly so angry, he thought he might explode. "No!" he shouted. "It's *not* cool. Not cool at all." He kicked a book across the floor.

Elizabeth's recoil made him even angrier. He could almost feel steam coming out of his ears, he was so furious. "What's it going to take? I don't know what else to do to prove to you that my feelings are genuine. I've brought you my grandmother's flowers. I've opened myself up and—and told you my hopes and dreams. I've risked humiliation by showing you the squalor I've been living in. Isn't that enough for you?"

Elizabeth tried to shrink into the couch, but William wouldn't let her. He grabbed her arm and leaned into her face. "Dr. Denby told me you'd understand. He said you *owed* me."

"Owed you? What are you talking about?" She squirmed beneath his gaze. "What did your psychiatrist say I owed you?"

"Dr. Denby *swore* to me that you would help me make things right. Don't you see? We have to be together forever to make up for . . . all the *bad* stuff . . . the pain, the hospital . . . the

245

humiliation . . . all my disappointment. Just look at me! Do I look like a happy person to you, Elizabeth?" He wiped his bad eye with the back of his free hand. "My life has been hell— all because of you. Don't you think I deserve a little happiness?"

He could see the candlelight reflecting in her tear-filled eyes, but making her cry wasn't enough. He had to make her understand. Taking a deep breath, he made an effort to soften his tone. "Don't cry, darling. I don't want you to cry, ever. I want you to be happy. I can make you happy. Can't you understand that?"

"Not really, William. I don't know what you're talking about."

William let go of her arm and collapsed beside her on the sofa. "Oh, it's hopeless. I'm so confused. . . . I'm messing this all up. When Dr. Denby explains it, it's all so clear."

"Well . . . ," Elizabeth said, edging away. "Maybe sometime I could talk to Dr. Denby. . . ."

William suddenly brightened. "Yes! That's an excellent idea. But would you really do that for me?"

"Sure." Elizabeth hugged the far arm of the couch and looked at him with sparkling, bright eyes. "You just name the time. From what you've told me, he sounds like a marvelous person. I'd be honored to meet someone who has helped you so much."

William jumped up and clapped. "You really mean it?"

"Yes, of course. When would you like me to meet him?"

He grabbed her hands and yanked her to her feet. "How about right now?"

"Th-This late?" Elizabeth stammered. "But won't Dr. Denby be asleep?"

"Dr. Denby is always available to me," William said, pulling roughly on her arms. "That's what makes him so special. He never turns me away. He lets me talk to him whenever I need him—no matter what time, day or night."

Elizabeth had been so terrified when William had started his ranting, she'd suggested a visit to Dr. Denby only to stall for time. She'd hoped that moving the subject away from their kiss might calm him enough to get him to lead her out of this awful place. Instead he was raving that they'd go see Dr. Denby *now*. She wanted to get away from William, not go to some insane asylum with him.

Elizabeth leaned back and tried to use her body leverage to break from his grasp. But William was too strong. Before she could break free, he was hauling her roughly across the floor.

He wasn't taking her to any doctor. What was he doing? She tried dragging her feet to stop his progress, but she couldn't get traction on the slick stone.

What happened to William's sweetness?

What happened to their beautiful night?

"Where are we going, William? The door is back that way!" Elizabeth craned her neck around toward the doorway where they'd entered the room. Suddenly she felt nauseous. The awful smell seemed to be getting worse.

"William, please. Let me go!"

"You said you'd talk to Dr. Denby."

"I will . . . tomorrow. I'll go see him first thing tomorrow, but now—"

"Tonight!" Still holding tightly to her wrist with one hand, William reached out with his free hand and opened a closet door. The overpowering smell that rolled out made Elizabeth gag. "You are going to talk to Dr. Denby *now*," William demanded. "You promised." He yanked a string, which turned on an overhead light in the closet.

Elizabeth screamed out every ounce of air she had in her lungs.

Dr. Denby—or what was left of him—lay slumped on the closet floor. Elizabeth was no forensic expert, but judging from the amount of decomposition, she'd say he'd been dead a long, long time.

Disgusting as it was, she couldn't take her eyes off the face. The darkened, leathery skin had stretched over the skull, giving the corpse a permanent grotesque smile. For a moment she thought she saw the flicker of an eyelash. Then a beetle of some sort skittered across the face to the shoulder, across the arm, and then dropped with a tiny plop off the tip of a bony, outstretched finger.

Elizabeth violently struggled to pull free from William's grasp. She thought her arm was going to come out of its socket.

Slowly William turned to face her. His eyes were glazed; his expression, peaceful and eerily calm. "Elizabeth, may I present Dr. Orrin Denby," he said with just a hint of a polite bow. "Dr. Denby, this is the girl I've been telling you about. This is my lovely Elizabeth Wakefield."

"Why, hello, Elizabeth."

Elizabeth gasped and choked for air.

"I'm so honored and happy to meet you," he continued. "You are even more beautiful than William has described. We're going to enjoy having you stay with us a long, long time."

Elizabeth shuddered at the sound of the deep, clipped, businesslike voice. But William just kept on talking for Dr. Denby, as if the rotting corpse were some psychotic ventriloquist's dummy.

Chapter
Fourteen

"She doesn't want to stay here with us, Dr. Denby," William said calmly. "She doesn't understand. Can you explain it to her? Please, can you make her understand?"

"What is it you don't understand, child?" Dr. Denby asked.

William pulled on Elizabeth's arm. "Come on, Elizabeth. You've got your chance. Now you can ask Dr. Denby whatever you want to know about me."

But Elizabeth just stood there with her hand mashed over her lovely lips and pert little nose.

"It's OK, Elizabeth. I understand if you feel shy about talking to a psychiatrist. I was too, at first. But it's the easiest thing in the world, really. Especially if the psychiatrist is a great man like Dr. Denby. Try it." He tugged harder, but Elizabeth seemed to be anchored to the floor.

He gave her a yank that caused her to stumble slightly, but still she resisted. "Don't be embarrassed. Dr. Denby already knows everything about us."

He turned back to Dr. Denby. "She doesn't understand how much I love her and how important it is for her to give herself to me completely. Can you convince her, Dr. Denby? Can you explain so she'll understand that we're supposed to be together forever?"

"Elizabeth, why are you so reluctant to commit to William?" Dr. Denby asked. "What he says is true, you know. He loves you more than anyone else could ever love you. You must love him equally for this to work. Give yourself to William—now—completely, for your own good."

Nodding in agreement, William turned back to Elizabeth. She stood there as pale as his mother's white roses, her aqua eyes as wide as saucers—frozen like a deer in headlights. Her sudden unwillingness to cooperate was starting to annoy him. "Don't look so horrified, Elizabeth," William said indulgently. "Dr. Denby won't hurt you. He wants you here. In fact, it was all Dr. Denby's idea to set up the virtual-reality fair. It used up the very last of my money, but it was worth it so I could show you how much I cared for you."

He pulled Elizabeth's hand away from her mouth so she could speak, but she didn't.

"Don't you appreciate my loving gesture? I did it all for you."

Elizabeth stumbled backward. William reached for her but missed.

"Hey, where are you going? Elizabeth. Don't run away! The doctor isn't finished with you yet! *Come back here!*"

With her stomach churning from the nauseating smell, Elizabeth bolted from William's room into the dank corridor. Her mind reeled in panic. She had no idea where she was going. She only knew she needed to get away.

"Don't go," she heard William yell behind her. "This is your home. You will get used to the dark after a while. It won't be so bad—not as long as we're together."

She hurried faster to escape the words she didn't want to hear.

"Forever, Elizabeth. We're meant to be together forever . . . dead or alive." His words echoed through the tunnel mercilessly. They seemed to come at her from all directions.

Suddenly three gaping black archways loomed in front of her. She'd hoped the Christmas lights would lead her away from William's lair, but each passageway had its own string of miserably weak, twinkling lights.

Which way? None of them looked familiar. But with William getting ever closer, she couldn't be choosy. She could hear his panting breath.

Left! she decided. She dashed down the left branch until it split, and then she turned left again. Unlike the corridor leading to the archives room, this passageway was hardly more than a narrow tunnel. The floors were hard-packed dirt, and she suspected the walls were too—but she wasn't about to touch them to find out. They were covered with mold, or moss, or something worse.

"You're going to get lost!" William shouted. "Don't you see how much you need me?"

Another left, then a right, and then she knew she was completely lost. But she had no choice but to keep going. If she turned back, she'd run right into William's arms. Nothing could be worse than that!

"Elizabeth, stop running from me." William's voice was becoming higher and more strained.

She ducked into a low-ceilinged passageway.

"Elizabeth, I won't stand for these silly games of yours," he screeched. "You're making me very angry!"

Elizabeth couldn't stop now. She had been so wrong. William White was still a homicidal, raving lunatic—if anything, he was worse than before.

"Elizabeth, don't make me have to punish you."

Suddenly the pathetic little string of lights flickered and went off. The tunnel was thrown into total blackness.

*   *   *

"There! Let's just see how well you do without electricity!" William's first yank had broken the electrical connection, but he didn't stop. In his rage he continued to tug on the strings of lights as if he were hauling in an anchor. Then, tossing the wad of cords into a pile, he charged onward. The darkness didn't bother him. He was used to it. After living below the library for months he knew all the tunnels like the back of his hand.

William made another left. Like an animal after its prey, he sniffed the air. He could practically smell her fear—tangy, spicy. It energized him.

He dove into a tunnel on his right. Pausing briefly, he turned his good ear in what he sensed was Elizabeth's direction. It was. In the distance he could hear her rapid breaths and her whimpering little mews echoing through the tunnel. He licked his lips and smiled.

"Here I come," he bellowed. He was beginning to enjoy the chase.

Somewhere not far away, he heard her bump into a wall. He cackled wildly. "Give up. You can't go on in the dark. It's hopeless. You're just wasting your time—and mine. Precious time we could be spending together."

"William!"

Her wavering voice floated back like music.

"William, can you hear me? Stop a minute. I need to ask you something."

William stopped. His mouth watered. He

wiped it with the back of his hand. "Ask me anything, my love."

"Why don't you let me go?" The question echoed back eerily.

William frowned. "That's impossible," he yelled. "It wouldn't fit my plan." He waited. When she didn't reply, he called to her again. "Aren't you curious? Don't you want to hear about my plan?" He cocked his good ear in her direction. She wasn't stopped. He could hear her footsteps scuttling through the tunnel. She was trying to trick him!

"I'm not amused!" he shrieked.

"I don't want to hear your plan!" Her voice sounded weaker. She was getting away!

William sped up. "Oh, but you're going to hear it anyway. I want you to know exactly what I'm going to do when I catch you." He grew more furious with each step. "When I catch you, I'm going to scar your face." His hand caressed his own scarred cheek.

He ran headlong into drooping cobwebs and brushed them aside. "I don't want to, but I have to," he continued. "Don't you see? Dr. Denby thinks your face must match mine for you to truly understand me."

William careened off a wall, but he never even slowed. "Don't worry. I'll be quick. It may hurt for a while, but not long. I couldn't bear to let you suffer *too* long. Just long enough for you to see what it's like . . . and then I'll slit your throat."

Her scream reverberated back to him. William leaned against the cool wall to catch his breath. The thought of watching Elizabeth's lifeblood drain from her body excited him. He would cleanse her of her old world, her old life, leaving her pure—for his world—forever.

Eagerly he resumed the chase. "You don't have to be afraid. You won't be alone. Not even in death. As soon as I'm sure you're dead, I'll join you," he shouted. "Dr. Denby doesn't know about that part. But I have to do it. I'll slit my own throat for you, Elizabeth. I *have* to . . . so we can be together forever and ever."

William gasped. There was another voice in the tunnel behind him.

"William . . ."

He slapped his hand over his good ear and crouched in the darkness. Dr. Denby! He'd heard everything! And he was angry—William could tell. Angry that he hadn't been completely honest with him.

"I'm sorry," William shouted back over his shoulder. "You can't help me anymore. All I need now is Elizabeth's love. For eternity."

"She will not be true, William. She's not worthy. She cannot be cleansed."

"No-o-o-o!" William shrieked. "You're lying to me. Elizabeth is mine. She's mine! Our love will never die!"

*　　*　　*

Elizabeth's side ached from running almost as much as her parched throat ached from panting. The tunnels went on and on. The endless darkness was driving her crazy. She was losing hope fast. She was actually going to die. She'd be propped up in William's closet, right next to Dr. Denby.

She leaned forward with her hands on her knees and gasped for air. The result was a gigantic sneeze. The stink of the rotting corpse still burned in her nose, and the air around her seemed thick with mold.

"Bless you, darling!" William's voice echoed from behind her. It spurred her back into motion. "I think it's time for you to give up now."

"Never!" she screamed with what little force she could muster. She had to keep going. She wasn't going to lie down and let William kill her. After all, she'd escaped from William White twice before. She could do it again.

Blindly she stumbled onward into the impenetrable darkness. She had no idea where she was going. She just knew that she didn't dare stop, not with the sound of that maniac ranting right behind her. Not only was he shouting at her, but from time to time she could hear him yelling at the nonexistent Dr. Denby.

Suddenly she crashed headlong into a wall. It sent her bouncing back a couple of steps and left her dizzy.

What did I hit? A dead end? She gave her head

a shake to clear it. Her heart pounded louder. *Keep your hands out,* she told herself.

She touched the wall and jerked back her hand. Visions of every sort of cavern-dwelling horror skittered across her mind—bugs, lizards, spiderwebs, bats, rats. . . . What was she about to touch? But did it really matter? Nothing she could imagine compared to the horror behind her.

She placed her palms flat against the cold, slimy wall and shuddered. She swallowed loudly, fighting down a wave of repulsion. Holding her breath, she felt her way to the left, where her fingers touched another wall at a right angle. She switched walls and groped her way along it. This time nothing stopped her. With each step she picked up a little confidence and a little speed. It hadn't been a dead end after all. The tunnel had simply made a sharp left turn. Keeping her left hand held out in front of her and letting her right hand trail lightly along the wall, Elizabeth stumbled on.

"Thank you, Dr. Denby." She heard William cackle. He sounded closer than ever. "Elizabeth . . . can you hear me? Dr. Denby is ready. He is going back for the knife."

Suddenly her outstretched hand smacked into another wall. Pain shot from her wrist to her shoulder. Was it another turn or a dead end this time?

Desperate, she groped her way along the wall

to a corner and another wall. No new tunnel opened up to save her. No way out. A dead end.

As she fumbled along the second wall to make sure, her foot hit something, causing her to stumble. Carefully she knelt down and felt along the cold, dank floor. Her fingers closed around something . . . a book.

Feeling her way back to the wall, she began to explore its surface with her fingers. "Ouch!" *A splinter?* She had touched wood. Then she felt something smooth and soft, but brittle—*leather?*

Her fingers flew, examining every inch of the surface within her reach. She was at a bookshelf. Could it possibly be *her* revolving bookshelf?

She carefully scooted her foot forward until she felt the familiar wooden step built into the case. Blindly she stumbled onto it and tried to position herself exactly the way she had before. Quickly she traced the edges of the wood until she found the latch.

She pulled.

Nothing happened. Her fingers were trembling so badly, she could hardly work the delicate mechanism.

"Dr. Denby is gone now, Elizabeth. It's just you and me." William was very close now. She could hear his raspy breath.

She yanked again. This time the latch clicked. She grabbed onto the shelf, letting it swing her into the familiar little room where she'd worked all week. It didn't matter that she was still in pitch darkness; she knew this had to be the archives room where she'd worked.

She eased to the left and stepped off the bookshelf riser. She stumbled. Waving her arms in front of her, she finally brushed against the wooden desk. She ran her hands lovingly across its surface. The top was still open, just the way she'd left it yesterday. There was the stack of papers she'd left in the corner.

She'd soon be free.

Flattening her back against the side of the desk, she struggled to get her bearings. If she took two giant steps from the desk and turned to her left, the doorway should be straight in front of her.

Letting go of the desk left her panicky for a moment. She felt disoriented, as if she'd closed her eyes and spun around. Holding her arms out like a sleepwalker in an old movie, she took two faltering steps and turned.

"Go for it," she coaxed herself. Taking a deep breath, she dashed across the open room.

She had to be close to the passageway now. But suddenly her foot was yanked out from under her and she tumbled to the hard floor. Her knees hit and then her hands. Jolting pains shot up her arms.

But who had tripped her? Elizabeth rolled over to one hip and kicked frantically but heard nothing—felt nothing. She was fighting air. No one, nothing was there.

With a groan she struggled back to her hands and knees and began to feel around on the floor. "Is anyone there?" she called. She held her breath and listened. Her own voice echoed around her. And then an insistent hissing sound.

A snake! Elizabeth snatched her hands back, horrified. But as she listened more closely, she realized it didn't really sound like a snake. More like air escaping from a balloon. Again she tentatively reached out and felt along the floor beside her. Her fingers bumped against the hard, cold pipe.

She had tripped over the gas pipe. And just as John Petrie had predicted, she'd broken it. She could actually feel the gas escaping from the pipe. She wrinkled her nose. She could smell it too. Gas was quickly filling the tiny chamber.

Holding her breath, Elizabeth grasped the door frame and pulled herself to her feet. She dashed into the familiar up-sloping, low-ceilinged corridor that she knew led to the library basement. Freedom was at hand, if she didn't suffocate first.

William smiled when he heard Elizabeth turn right into the old library passage. The chase was coming to an end. She was headed straight for nowhere. He'd been down this way many times and knew this corridor dead-ended at the old bookshelf.

He instinctively slowed his steps, knowing that he was nearing the end of the tunnel. He was so close to his prize now, he could hardly breathe from excitement.

"Where are you, my precious?" He paused and held out his arms the way a child does when playing blindman's bluff. His fingers brushed the cool, damp wall on his right. "There's no place to hide. This tunnel you've chosen is a dead end. Dead. Get it?"

He felt to the left—again, nothing but smooth, cool stone beneath his fingers. He stopped and listened. No matter how hard he tried, he could no longer hear her ragged breath. "You can't hold your breath forever, Elizabeth. And you can't hide!" He imagined her leaning against the wall, frozen like a statue, hoping to avoid detection.

"You're only stalling the inevitable, my love." He paused, waiting to see if she'd make a break for it. Nothing. He moved to the left side of the corridor and patted his hands along the wall. When it ended, he ran his hand across the old wooden bookcase, feeling the ripples of book after book. Then he felt wood again, then stone again, and then the right-hand wall.

He let out an infuriated snarl like a trapped animal. She couldn't have gotten past him. The corridor was so narrow, he would have felt her pass or at least heard her.

Had he been mistaken? Had she not come this way? As he sank to the steps of the old bookshelf, his hand brushed something soft. He felt along the floor until his fingers closed around the object. He brought it to his nose. It smelled fresh and sweet, like Elizabeth. It was her sweater. He'd been right all along. She *had* come this way. So how did she get away?

Overcome with anger and frustration, he beat his fists against the bookshelf. When that didn't appease his anger, he began pulling books from the shelf and throwing them. "Elizabeth!" he screamed as he tossed book after book into the dark corridor. "Where are you?"

He sobbed. She couldn't have vanished into thin air. And there couldn't be a trapdoor he didn't know about. He'd seen the blueprints. He knew these tunnels inside and out. He snarled and turned in a useless circle. Did the tunnels hold secrets even he hadn't yet discovered? The possibility existed, and he knew it.

"A latch. There's got to be a latch here. There's got to be!" But he couldn't wait to feel it out with his hands. He needed light.

He slapped at his khakis, trying to remember which pocket he'd dropped the lighter into. "There it is!" But his fingers were trembling so violently, it slipped from his grasp. Cursing, he dropped to his hands and knees and felt around on the floor. "Ah! Here it is," he whispered as his fingers closed around the cheap plastic. With the practiced familiarity of an ex-chain-smoker, he grasped the lighter and flicked it—

After leaving the television station Tom had stopped by his dorm to shower and change clothes. He wanted Elizabeth to know he was making every effort to impress her. There had seemed to be no need to hurry, but as he strode toward the library, an odd, frightening feeling of déjà vu swept over him. For a moment he felt all tingly and full of adrenaline—exactly the way he'd felt in his CyberDream when he was being called to rescue his princess.

He looked around campus and saw no reason for his alarm. It was a typical Friday night. Somewhere in the distance he could hear music coming from one of the fraternity houses. All around him couples were walking hand in hand, taking advantage of the clear, crisp evening.

Although the leaves were so still, they could have been painted on the trees, Tom distinctly felt a breeze across his face. Something was wrong. The hairs on the back of his neck prickled.

His steps involuntarily speeded to a jog. He panted as he broke into a run. Faster. Faster.

Just as he crossed the quad, an unidentifiable muffled *wham!* brought his feet up to his knees.

He dropped down on all fours. *Earthquake?* he wondered. The ground trembled beneath him. He heard glass breaking and a sound like a mountain ripping in two.

The ringing in his ears died down. The rumble stopped. He heard a scream. Students were running across the quad. All headed toward the library.

Tom turned toward the tall, stately building. At first it seemed as if all the lights were on and all was well. But then Tom realized that the orange light glowing behind the library windows flickered unnaturally. Smoke curled upward from the very foundation.

As if he were watching some bizarre movie, Tom saw the night security officers fleeing from the library's front door. "Call nine-one-one," he heard one of them shout to a bystander with a cell phone. "There's been an explosion in the library—the basement, we think."

Elizabeth! Tom struggled to his feet. Heedless of the danger, he raced with renewed effort toward the wide glass doors of the library.

"Hey, you! Get away from there!" someone shouted.

Just before Tom reached the library's steps, someone tackled him around the waist and sent him sprawling into a flower bed.

"You can't go in there, man," a campus security guard barked in Tom's ear. He helped Tom to his feet but didn't release his grip. "There's been an explosion. The whole place is on fire."

Elizabeth crouched behind a thick old card catalog as flames erupted around her. Her eyes were burning. Her lungs felt as if they were on fire. And now it was starting to rain.

Rain? In the library basement?

The thick, black smoke had her so woozy and disoriented, it took her several seconds to realize that the sprinkler system had kicked on. She looked toward the ceiling with relief. But after the initial icy deluge came a trickle. Then it stopped.

The sprinklers weren't working.

Elizabeth wiped the water out of her eyes. She stood up and turned around in a circle. Lack of oxygen was quickly taking away her ability to reason. She had to escape fast, or it would be too late.

But where was the exit? She'd already given up on the old boiler room and William's secret exit—she'd have to backtrack through the smoke. She was going to have to try for the main library exit on the first floor and just hope it wouldn't be locked. But first she'd have to make it to the stairwell. That is, if she could just get her bearings and *find* the stairwell. Once she made it that far, she should be OK. Weren't they designed to be fireproof?

She had stumbled as far as the nearest

bookshelf when a sudden fit of coughing brought her to her knees. She reached for Jessica's sweater to hold over her mouth, but it was gone. "Oh, Jess is going to be so mad at me," she whispered groggily.

Think! her brain screamed. *Stay focused. There's no time to spare.*

Elizabeth tried . . . but it was so hard. She recognized where she was. She had made it as far as the English-lit stacks. It couldn't be far to the stairs . . . but . . .

Elizabeth's concentration broke as she was distracted by the books. All around her they were starting to smolder and curl from the intense heat. She felt like crying. What an incredible waste. All those beautiful books!

There was a crash nearby. A shelf gave way and books rained down. Sparks flew through the black haze in a brief orange shower. A smoldering ember dropped on her arm. She yelped and brushed it away. The shock brought her back to the matter at hand—escaping the inferno.

Stay low, some drilled-in, instinctive voice from grade-school fire drills commanded. *Look for emergency exit signs. Crawl out of the building.*

With her hands over her face Elizabeth hunched over and lurched through the smoke and flames in the direction she hoped led to the stairwell.

She bumped into the old Naugahyde sofa. It

too was starting to smolder. She groped for the magazine rack . . . the concrete-block wall . . . the light switch. The exit light should be just around the corner. But it wasn't.

Elizabeth waved an arm in front of her and inched forward. Finally her fingers grazed the opposite wall. And just when she thought she couldn't hold her breath another second, the big green steel door of the stairwell loomed in front of her.

Cautiously she reached out and touched it. It wasn't hot—not that she could tell anyway. Not when everything else around her felt like ground zero in a blast furnace.

The effort it took to pull the heavy door open sent her into another fit of coughing, but she staggered inside the stairwell and let the door slam behind her. She'd never been so glad to see the ugly concrete steps and the uglier metal slip guards and handrails.

The emergency-exit sign, though far overhead, was a godsend. The stairwell was full of smoke, but there were no visible flames. She stepped on the first step and wobbled dizzily. It was only one flight. Surely she could make it.

She took two more steps before giving out completely. She lay there in a daze. Every inch of her body ached. The stairs loomed ahead of her like Mount Everest.

"Tom," she muttered.

She laid her face against the concrete step and let her tears fall. Once she'd heard a fireman talking about how many fire victims were found within feet of the door. "Not me," she whispered hoarsely. "Not me."

Clinging to the rail, she pulled herself back to her feet. Then hand over hand she pulled herself up the stairs to the library's main floor.

Bursting into the main level of the library, she found it better lit but full of hazy black smoke. It looked like some alien planet with low-hanging clouds of unbreathable atmosphere. But through the haze she could make out the wide glass doors lit from the campus lights outside.

Holding her breath, she stumbled toward them. Her hands reached the glass. She waited for it to open. Nothing. She pushed. Still nothing.

The automatic doors weren't working. Safety was just beyond the glass, and she couldn't get to it.

She beat against the door with her fists. Sweat trickled down her face. Then she remembered that there was another door—a side door. A door that wasn't automatic.

She clambered over the turnstile to the narrow door on the end. Praying it wasn't locked, she threw her weight against the bar. It popped open with a resounding clunk, and she burst free from the smoke-filled prison.

Freedom! She closed her burning eyes and

sucked in a great gasp of fresh air—glorious fresh air . . . which she choked on as a pair of strong arms suddenly grabbed her.

William had survived.

She struggled. Pummeling William's face with weak blows, she screamed with the last of the air in her scalded lungs.

"Elizabeth, stop struggling." He wrestled her to the sidewalk.

With her eyes squeezed shut, she continued to flail her arms.

"You're safe. It's me . . . ," Tom cried, not even trying to dodge her pathetic blows.

"Tom?" She went as limp as a rag doll in his arms. "Tom. Oh, Tom, it really *is* you." She immediately burst into relieved tears and collapsed against him.

"I'm here now." He stroked her hair with one hand while holding her tight with the other.

She looked up at him, her big, blue-green eyes rimmed in red. "I'm so—" The effort to speak sent her into a spasm of coughing.

He held her more tightly.

"I'm sorry," she croaked when she recovered her breath. "So, so very sorry."

"Shhh—don't try to talk."

Suddenly there was a loud crash. Glass rained around them as an upstairs window exploded from the intense heat.

"Come on—we've got to get away from here. We're still too close to the fire." He helped her to her feet and half carried, half guided her out to the quad.

"It's so cool," she cried, sinking to her knees and grabbing a handful of the wet grass. "So heavenly cool."

Sitting down beside her, he pulled her into his arms and kissed the top of her disheveled hair. It smelled like the inside of a dirty barbecue pit, but he didn't care. Just as long as she was safe.

"Hold me," she whispered, clinging to him like a kitten.

"I am," he said, holding her as tightly as his trembling arms would allow. He was almost afraid that if he loosened his grip, she might fly away. "You're safe now. I've got you."

"It—it was so awf—" Her voice broke. She buried her face against his shirt and began to cry uncontrollably.

"What happened?" Tom asked when her sobbing slowed to an occasional sniff. "Do you know what caused the explosion?"

He could feel her nodding against his chest. "William," she said, lifting her soot-covered face to his.

"William? William who?" He looked at her pained expression and felt the blood drain from his own face. Again he was filled with a horrible déjà vu—only this time it had nothing to do with virtual reality. He was suddenly reliving a near-death experience on a winding mountain road after a football game. "Not William White," he gasped, not wanting to believe it himself.

"Yes," Elizabeth admitted weakly. "He wasn't killed in the wreck like we'd thought. He's been here on campus for weeks—maybe longer. After that awful CyberDreams fair—I thought I was going crazy. He told me he'd come back for me. . . ."

"When was this? Sunday? The day I knocked myself out on the quad?" Tom touched the back of his still tender head. "I didn't run into a limb. William—he must have knocked me unconscious." Tom reeled with the news.

Suddenly the whole week swam into focus. No wonder Elizabeth had been acting so strangely. He cupped her precious face in his hands. "Why didn't you tell me?"

"I couldn't. I was too afraid—"

"You can always confide in me. We're supposed to be partners, remember? Don't cut me out of your life."

"Oh, Tom, I'm so sorry . . . forgive me?"

"Shhh, don't be silly." The pleading look in her eyes nearly broke his heart. Here she had almost been killed, and she was asking *him* for forgiveness. "Don't you know I'd forgive you absolutely anything? Nothing else matters now." He pulled her tight against his chest again and sobbed against her hair. "Nothing."

Through his tear-filled eyes he watched the quad fill with the flashing red and blue of fire trucks, police cars, and ambulances. He heard their wailing sirens and the voices of the men shouting directions at one another. He even vaguely noticed the buzzing chatter of the onlookers who'd gathered around the fringes of the quad to watch the flames and smoke roll from the library.

Suddenly someone tapped Tom on the shoulder. Without relinquishing his hold on Elizabeth he craned his neck to look up into the face of a campus policeman.

"Excuse me. An ambulance is here. Do either of you need medical attention?"

Tom looked questioningly into Elizabeth's face. "I feel OK," she insisted. "But I guess I should get checked out . . . just to be safe."

"Is either of you a witness to what happened here?"

"I—I am," Elizabeth admitted as Tom helped her to her feet.

"We're going to need some information from you," the policeman said. He tailed the couple all the way to the ambulance.

Elizabeth sneezed loudly and began to cough again.

Tom wrapped his arm protectively back around her. "Can't you let her get taken care of first? It's chilly out here. And she's been through an awful lot. She's inhaled smoke and . . . who *knows* what else."

"I'll tell you everything," Elizabeth croaked. "My name is Elizabeth Wakefield, and I just live right over there in Dickenson Hall. Room twenty-eight," she added with a sniff.

"OK. You go ahead and get checked out." He jotted the information on a small pad. "I'll be over to talk to you in an hour."

Tom helped her into the ambulance.

"Oh," Elizabeth said, turning back to the policeman. "Could you please contact Detective Bart Kaydon of the Sweet Valley precinct? I think he'll want to be in on this."

Chapter
Fifteen

"That's all I can tell you," Elizabeth said, quietly finishing her statement to Detective Kaydon and the campus policeman who had accompanied him to her room. The words had come much easier than she'd expected. It'd helped that Tom's arms were still securely around her shoulders.

"I don't think you have anything to worry about anymore, Miss Wakefield," the campus policeman said. "There's no way anyone down in those tunnels could have survived that blast—the place is a broiling inferno even now. I heard one fireman say it could be weeks, maybe months, before it'll be safe to go down below ground level."

Detective Kaydon twisted his hat between his hands. "We're sorry for the trauma you've suffered, Elizabeth. We had no idea that William had escaped from Dr. Denby's clinic, or even that Dr. Denby was dead."

Elizabeth stiffened as an angry flush came over her. A not so very nice version of "I told you so" was on the tip of her tongue, but she was just too tired to pursue it. Instead she simply nodded.

"I have officers checking into the details right now," he continued. "All we know so far is that his secretary and nurse were given sudden paid vacations and his partner was told that Dr. Denby was on an extended leave for health reasons. The exact manner of Denby's death—well, I don't think we'll be able to determine that now. The underground corridors are destroyed, fire officials tell me. It's doubtful there'll be anything left of Dr. Denby—or William White either. I guess we'll never know."

Elizabeth leaned against Tom and yawned.

"OK. We'll be going now," Detective Kaydon said, urging the campus policeman toward the door. "Call us if you remember anything else. And again, I hope you accept our sincerest apology."

After the police left, Tom fluffed up a couple of pillows and eased Elizabeth back onto them. "It's nearly three. Try to get some rest."

She reached up, grabbed his shirt, and pulled him down beside her. "Stay with me."

"Gladly." He situated himself on the bed and sighed.

She snuggled against him. "I don't know if I can ever stand to be alone again."

"Liz, it's OK now. The nightmare is over," Tom

said, kissing her lips tenderly. He reached over to her desk and picked up the wet cloth he'd laid there earlier. Gently he dabbed her swollen eyes. "And soon things will be better than they ever were."

She took the cloth from his hands and dropped it on the floor. "I don't care about better," she said, cupping his face in her hands. "I just want things to get back to normal."

Suddenly there was a scratching at the door. The doorknob jiggled wildly.

"It's him!" Elizabeth screamed. She jumped to her feet, sending Tom sprawling to the floor.

Tom scrambled to his feet and braced his body protectively in front of Elizabeth's.

The door flew open with a bang. "Elizabeth!" Jessica shouted as she bounded inside. "I have had the most exciting night of my entire life! I saw absolutely everybody who was anybody!" She unwound her purple shawl and tossed it toward her bed. "Remember Brandon Hunter, that hunky actor from *The Young and the Beautiful*—the one who dated me that time, just thinking I could advance his career? You should have seen his face when he saw me tonight. Positively green. He couldn't stand it!"

Elizabeth opened her mouth, but Jessica charged on without giving her a space to speak.

"And Charles . . . if you thought he was gorgeous two years ago, you should have seen him tonight. His hair has gotten kinda longish, and he had on an Armani tux, and we looked absolutely *stunning* together. Everyone was asking me about my necklace—"

Tom unwound himself from Elizabeth and cleared his throat noisily.

"*What?*" Jessica asked, not bothering to hide her annoyance at being interrupted. "Why are you two looking at me that way?" she asked cluelessly. "Is my makeup smeared or something?" She leaned toward the mirror and checked her lipstick.

"Jessica, aren't you the least bit concerned about why your sister is sitting here with smoke-smudged cheeks and dripping-wet hair?" Tom asked.

"Oh, is she? I hadn't noticed." Jessica glanced briefly in their direction and turned back to her own reflection in the mirror. Running her hand along the lines of her purple gown, she smiled dreamily. "Anyway, as I was saying . . . *Checkered Houses* actually won the IMA for best movie! And when Charles went up onstage to accept, he thanked *me!* Of course he mentioned a bunch of boring other people too, but isn't that a maximum thrill?"

Elizabeth looked at Tom and burst out laughing. "Wait—did I say I wanted things to get back to normal?" she asked him. "I actually meant—"

"Don't tell me," Tom said. "You meant . . . this." And he lowered his lips to hers.

Check out the **all-new**....

..........(Sweet Valley Web site—)

www.sweetvalley.com

New Features

Cool Prizes

The **ONLY** official Web site!

Hot Links

....(And much more!)

BFYR 202